Hope - A World Divided

By

Jake Phillips

ISBN: 9781916981348

Chapter 1

Beginning of Time

Long ago, in the beginning of time, the world was still young. The world was one and united, there were no barriers separating the land. The rivers flowed freely, connecting the different parts of the land, the oceans were calm and serene. The forests were lusciously green and thriving. The world was a peaceful place. Although the world was united there were four distinct regions, vast and diverse from one another.

The first region, Earnoche, was the Northern most land that had a vast forest that stretched for miles, filled with towering trees and lush greenery. It was a place of magic and wonder, where the trees and greenery were at its most beautiful.

The second region, Cravmod, which lay to the East, was a dangerously rugged and mountainous region, filled with steep cliffs and deep caves. Although this region was a dangerous place is was a magnificent sight to behold.

The Southernmost region, Postis, was land filled with vast ocean, filled with crystal-clear waters and colourful coral reefs. It was a place of beauty and grace, where the waves would glide care free.

To the West was Wyvinite, it was a fertile plain, filled with lush crops and grasslands. It was a place high among the clouds. It was peaceful, all you could hear were gentle gushes of wind flowing through the air.

These four distinct regions would later be home to four different races: the Elvians, Mountaineers, Aquanauts, and Wyvinites.

But how these races and regions became to be is a story in itself.

Chapter 2

The Cataclysm

On a cold day, in the heights of winter, 3000 years ago, the beautiful trees of Earnoche began to sway. The Snow began to settle on the mountains of Cravmod. The wonderfully blue waters of Postis changed from being delicately still to waves crashing the shore. The wind was hurling past the volcanic mountains of Wyvinite.

The worst storm this world had ever seen was beginning to take place. The first of many natural disasters struck! A massive earthquake shook the land. The earthquake was so powerful that it created deep chasms and towering mountains and cliffs. The earthquake created multiple tsunamis all around the land. The once clear and beautiful ocean rose and engulfed the low-lying areas, separating the regions and isolating the different parts of the land from each other.

Lashes of lighting continuously struck creating huge flames and embers all over. These fires burnt down every tree in its way. The destruction of this once precious land was ruined.

The northern region, Earnoche, was now trapped. Once there was a lush green vast forest. The earthquake ripped every tree up from once it stood and the fires tore through and burned the once scenic forest into an ashy black nothingness. All that remained were towering cliffs, raging rivers and burnt land.

The eastern region, Cravmod, was trapped on a baron plain, surrounded by the driest and scorching vast sandy desert and towering icy mountains. This was a treacherous emptiness landscape.

The southernmost region of Postis, was trapped in the middle of an ocean, surrounded by towering waterfalls and unforgiving currents. You would look out to the horizon as far as you could, there was nothing, nothing but deep dark ocean.

The western region, Wyvinite, was now trapped. The region was imprisoned by massive lava flowing volcanic mountains.

Wyvinite had been cut off from the rest of the world by a deep and ghastly chasm surrounding it.

The only living things at this point were the spirits of the elements, who roamed the land, shaping it to their will.

Chapter 3

The Elvian New Beginning

3000 years later, it was just another dark and miserable day, everything was bleak, and everything was gone. The only things that remained in Earnoche was a spirit of the air. This spirit was wondering around Earnoche rather glumly, this was understandable, as there was nothing left. The spirit stumbled across something rather outstandingly. The Spirit came across a small seedling! This small seedling was struggling to survive in the harshest of environments. The spirit seeing this seedling struggle, automatically felt a deep mothering connection to it, and decided to stay and try and protect and nurture it. Returning every day to protect this seedling, the days and months passed, the seedling grew into a magnificent tree, and the spirit realised that this tree was a symbol of life and hope in a world that had none for thousands of years.

As the tree grew over time, other spirits of the elements were told about this progress and had to come and see it for themselves. Once they saw this tree they also immediately felt a protective connection to it. All the spirits of the elements decided to work together to protect and nurture the tree the best they could. Over time as they were protecting and nurturing the tree, the tree known as The Tree of Life, they soon realised that more trees were beginning to sprout up around it. They could not believe this was happening. Their hard work and dedication to this tree was paying off.

As the trees grew over time, they brought life back to the land. At this point the spirits realised that they had created something truly remarkable and special. The air spirits made a bold decision that they thought was best, to take the land of Earnoche back to its former glory days. They decided to take on a physical form to live among

Chapter 4

The Mountaineers New Beginning

In the depths of the earth, in the dark and cavernous depths of the mountains, the Mountaineers came to be. They were born of the earth itself, forged in the fiery depths of the earth's core.

It was just another day in Cravmod, the rumbles from the land below the creaking and echoing from one mountain side to the next. There were rumbles from deep within the mountains and a loud thunderous bang, the mountains shook. The earth's core put so much pressure on the mountains from beneath, rocks started to smash against the peaks. The spirits of the earth could not bear to see any more destruction. So the Spirits of the earth made their way to the peak and clasped onto the exploding rocks. The sound almost like thunder and a bright light blinded the region. When the bright light dimmed you could see that the Mountaineers were born.

The Mountaineers looked small but hardy and resilient. They were made of strength almost as hard as stone and steel, and they were unyielding in the face of adversity. The Mountaineers had an instant connection with not only the earth they walked on but the mountains, they believed they had a debt to the earth and mountains as it had formed them. The Mountaineers tried their best to repay the earth and mountains by learning everything there was to learn about the mountains they now inhabited.

Chapter 5

The Aquanauts New Beginning

The Aquanauts were a race of creatures that lived on the land near the deep, mysterious depths of the ocean. They were born of the sea, and they were as much a part of it as the fish that swam alongside them. They were a graceful and beautiful race, with skin that shimmered like the ocean itself, and they were as mysterious as the depths they called home.

The Aquanauts were born in the ocean, and they knew the secrets of the sea. They knew how to find the hidden caves and grottoes that held the rarest and most precious gems and pearls. They were the only race that knew how to extract these precious resources, and they knew that it was vital to their survival.

These Aquanauts were formed after the earthquake caused a huge tsunami that crashed into everything in its path on the way to Postis. The tsunami left a trail of dead marine life. The water spirits appeared and was shocked and distraught at their discovery. The pain grew too much, so they decided to transform the dead marine life into only a few living Aquanauts.

Chapter 6

The Wyvinites New Beginning

The Wyvinites were a race of powerful and majestic creatures that lived in the fertile and ashy volcanic mountains. They were raised from the lava by the fire spirits, and they were as fierce and wild as the flames that danced within their hearts. They were a proud and noble race, with wings on their back that soared through the skies.

The Wyvinites were born in the ashy volcanic mountains, and they knew the secrets of the earth. They knew how to find the fertile soil that was perfect for growing crops, and they knew how to tend to them. They were the only race that knew how to cultivate the land for crops, and they knew that it was vital to their survival.

Chapter 7

Alone?

8

Each of these lands was separated by vast distances and natural barriers such as treacherous mountains, fast flowing rivers, dense green forests and wide and relentless oceans. These barriers ensured each race was isolated from each other and they were unaware of the existence of the other races. They had lived in these isolated regions for countless centuries now, each believing that they were the only intelligent living race alive in this lonely world.

Each race had their own myths and legends about the world beyond their own lands, but they had never had any contact with the other races, and so they had no way of knowing that if the myths were true or not.

Chapter 8

The Elvian Forest

Some time had passed and now the Elvians are now surrounded by towering trees and dense foliage to live in. As time raged on they learned more and more each day. They learnt how to use the wood from the trees to build their magnificent homes and create basic tools for their daily lives. They had discovered that the trees helped with water collection. They created a unique tool that allowed them to catch the water from the leaves and store it in wooden containers protected by strong green leaves.

As much as anyone would have thought this forest was a paradise, from a quick glance. They would have been wrong. This forest, although blooming with life now, only had a limited number of fruit trees. The Elvians had to take extra care of the remarkable fruit trees to ensure their survival. They created a spectacular system of irrigation, using the water from the leaves to water the trees and keep them healthy. They also developed methods to protect the trees from the elements, such as building shelters and creating barriers to block the sometimes unforgiving wind.

The Elvians learned that the trees were their most valuable resource and their survival depended on them. They dedicated their lives to the care and protection of the trees, and they passed down their knowledge from generation to generation. The Elvians had become masters of the forest, and their expertise in the use of wood and water was unmatched. They learned to live in harmony with nature, and the forest became their home, their source of food and water, and their greatest treasure.

Chapter 9

The Mountain Kingdom

The mountaineers lived in a rugged and inhospitable region, surrounded by towering peaks, deep valleys and scorching desert. They were hardy people, used to living in these extreme conditions, and they relied on their strength and cunning to survive. As a result of these living conditions over centuries they learned how to use the ore that was abundant in their mountains to create tools such as metal tipped spears for hunting and pickaxes for mining amongst other tools for everyday use.

The mountaineers built their homes in the cliffs, using the ore to create sturdy structures that could withstand the harsh winds and storms that relentlessly hit. The Mountaineers also created a sophisticated system to harness the steam from the hot ore veins and turn it into drinking water. They drilled tunnels into the mountains and built machines to convert the steam into a clean and safe source of water.

The mountaineers were known for their cunning and their ability to survive in harsh conditions. They became experts in the use of ore, and they created weapons and tools that were unmatched in quality and strength. They developed a unique hunting style, using their skills and the tools they created to bring down the biggest and most dangerous creatures that roamed their mountains.

Chapter 10

The Gem Kingdom

Centuries had passed since the major catastrophe hit. The Aquanauts now lived in a region that was surrounded by the vast and mysterious ocean. They were graceful and curious people, always exploring their environment and learning its secrets. They discovered that the pearls and jewels that were abundant in their seas were not only beautiful, but also useful. They learned how to harness the light of the sun through the jewels to create fire, which they used for warmth and cooking. However, there was not an abundance of wood on their lands.

The Aquanauts built their homes on the coral reefs, using the pearls and jewels to create stunning structures that glimmered in the light of the sun. They also learned how to hunt their waters for fish. Using their expert knowledge of the ocean and their finely crafted gem fishing tools. They were peaceful people, and they lived in harmony with the sea and its creatures.

Chapter 11

The Dragons Lair

The Wyvinites have lived in the ashy volcanic region of Wyvinite for multiple years after the New Beginning and have developed techniques for irrigation and crop rotation, ensuring that their fields remain productive year after year.

The Wyvinites have a small close-knit community, and they work together to maintain their farms and take care of each other. They are proud and fiery people, and they value the traditions that have been passed down through the generations.

Every day, the Wyvinites rise with the sun and start their day by tending to their crops. They spend hours gliding around their fields, planting, cultivating, and harvesting the crops that are essential to their survival. They take great care to preserve the soil and to keep it fertile with the help of the volcanos, knowing that their future depends on the health of their fields.

In the evenings, the Wyvinites gather in their communal halls to share stories, play music, and dance. They celebrate the beauty of the land and their connection to it, and they reinforce their bonds as a community.

For the Wyvinites, the land is life itself, and they will stop at nothing to protect it and ensure its prosperity. Their days are filled with hard work, but they are also filled with joy and purpose, as they work to preserve the traditions and way of life that have sustained them for so many generations.

Chapter 12

Kraken and the Mountaineers

Norakor a wise old man and Dugruck, two of the Mountaineers, were sitting in front of a group of little young Mountaineers, eager to hear the tale they had to tell. Norakor and Dugruck were well-respected members of their community and known for their storytelling skills, especially when it came to the myths and legends of Kraken.

The little ones sat in awe, their eyes wide open as Norakor and Dugruck began to tell the story of Kraken. Norakor began;

"Once upon a time, in the depths of the sea, there lived a monster known as Kraken," Norakor began, his deep voice echoing through the small room. "The Kraken was a giant creature, with tentacles that could reach the length of entire ships. It was said that if you saw Kraken, you were doomed to a watery grave."

Dugruck picked up the story, his gruff voice adding to the dramatic effect. "But the Kraken wasn't always a monster. In fact, it was once a beautiful creature, loved by all the sea creatures. But one day, the Kraken made a mistake. It allowed its anger and hatred to consume it, and it became the monster we all know today."

The little ones shuddered, imagining the terrifying Kraken in their minds.

"But the Mountaineers are not afraid of Kraken," Norakor said with a grin. "We have the strongest ore in the world and the best miners. We use it to make our weapons and our tools, and we are prepared to defend ourselves against any monster that comes our way."

Dugruck leaned in. "That's why we tell this story to the little ones. To remind them of the power of the ore, and the strength of the Mountaineers. We may be small, but we are mighty in spirit."

The little ones cheered and clapped, happy to hear such a thrilling story from Norakor and Dugruck. They went to bed that night, dreaming of Kraken and the strength of the Mountaineers, knowing that they too could one day be brave and strong like Norakor and Dugruck.

Chapter 13

The Endless Horizon

The warm glow of the pearls and jewels scattered around the fire illuminated the faces of the Aquanauts gathered together. Triton, the leader of the Aquanauts, sat cross-legged on the beach, surrounded by his trusted advisors Zale and Naia, and the curious Roka.

Zale leaned forward, his keen eyes reflecting the light of the fire. "What do you think lies beyond the horizon, Triton?" he asked, his voice low with wonder.

Triton sighed, running his hand through his hair. "It's a question that's plagued us for generations, Zale," he said. "Some say there's nothing out there, just endless ocean and darkness. Others believe there's a whole other world waiting for us to discover it."

Naia leaned in, her eyes alight with excitement. "I've heard stories of creatures we've never seen, of lands made of gold and silver," she said, her voice filled with wonder also.

Roka gave a warm smile. "I've always wanted to see what's out there," he said, his voice filled with longing. "But I'm scared. What if there's something dangerous waiting for us?"

At that moment, a young Aquanaut named Toru approached the fire. He had been listening from a distance, his curiosity piqued by the conversation.

Triton noticed him and smiled. "Toru, come join us," he said, patting the spot next to him.

Toru hesitated for a moment before approaching the fire, his eyes wide with wonder. "What are you all talking about?" he asked.

Triton chuckled. "We're discussing the unknown," he said. "The possibilities that lie beyond the horizon."

Toru's eyes lit up. "I want to see what's out there," he said, his voice filled with determination.

Triton nodded, his eyes filled with pride. "Maybe someday, Toru, you'll be the one to discover what lies beyond the horizon."

The Aquanauts sat in silence for a moment, each lost in their own thoughts about the endless possibilities waiting for them beyond the horizon. It was a mystery that would remain unsolved for now, but one day, perhaps, an Aquanaut would have the courage to venture out and uncover its secrets.

Chapter 14

The Aquanauts' Dilemma

It was a cold and dreary day in the kingdom of Postis. The once lively and bustling community was now filled with worry and fear. As they were noticeably running out of driftwood to burn for heat, and it seemed the water was becoming colder by the day.

Triton, the leader of the Aquanaut community, sat around the dwindling fire with his second in command, Zale, and Zale's wife, Naia. Roka, a seasoned Aquanaut who was the lead tracker for drift wood, was also present.

"What are we going to do?" Zale asked, worry etched on his face. "The young ones are already starting to suffer from the cold."

Triton sighed, rubbing his chin. "We may have to send out a party to gather more wood and see what's out there, but it might not be easy. The oceans current is stronger than ever, and it's dangerous to venture out alone."

Roka spoke up. "If and when we leave I can lead a group. I've been through the current before."

Triton Acknowledged. "That's good of you, Roka. We'll need all the help we can get."

Just then, a commotion could be heard from outside the food hut. Triton and the others quickly went to investigate. They found Nixie, a young Aquanaut, standing outside with a look of anger on her face.

"What's going on here?" Triton asked.

"It's Toru," Nixie said, pointing to a young Aquanaut standing nearby. "I caught him stealing fish from the food hut."

Toru's face turned red with embarrassment and anger. "I didn't steal anything," he lied.

Nixie scoffed. "You're a liar, Toru. I saw you with my own two eyes."

Triton frowned, looking at Toru. "Is this true?"

Toru hung his head, unable to look Triton in the eyes. "Yes," he whispered.

Triton sighed. "This is a serious matter, Toru. Stealing from the food hut endangers the entire community. I'll have to think about what to do with you."

Zale and Naia shared a worried look, while Roka just shook her head in disappointment. Toru was now known as a liar, and his actions could have serious consequences for the entire community.

Chapter 15

Meet The Lizards

The Lizard Monsters were described as creatures from the darkest shadows, with green scaly skin, razor sharp teeth and glowing red eyes. The Lizard Monsters were frightening and lived in the darkest shadows, deep within caves and crevices. They were elusive creatures, and rarely seen.

There were stories along with memories of these creatures and everyone knew that they were incredibly dangerous. Some argued that they could not afford to ignore the monsters and some say they should.

They were feared by most, there were tales of their hunting prowess and insatiable appetite for anything that crossed their path. Despite their reputation, however, very little was truly known about the lizard monsters and their mysterious ways. They remained a constant enigma, lurking in the shadows, waiting for their next prey.

Chapter 16

Monster Scouting Mission

The Lizard monsters were a curious, cunning species, always eager to explore and gather information about the other creatures that lived outside of the darkness.

One day, the leader of the monsters, T'kal, sent out a scout team to observe the Elvian and Wyvinites. The team was comprised of only a few of the swiftest and stealthiest lizard monsters, each with their own unique abilities and strengths.

As the monsters crept through the shadows, they watched the Elvians and Wyvinites going about their daily routines. They observed the way the Elvians tended to their sacred trees, carefully nurturing each one and protecting it from harm. They saw the way the Wyvinites worked the fertile land, planting and harvesting crops with a deep understanding of the cycles of life and growth.

The monsters noted all of these details, cataloguing them in their minds and storing the information away for future reference. They also kept a keen eye out for any weaknesses or vulnerabilities that they might be able to exploit.

Once their scouting mission was complete, the monsters returned to T'kal, eager to share what they had learned. The leader listened intently, nodding in approval as they heard of the observations made by the scout team.

"Well done," T'kal said. "This information will be invaluable to us as we continue our quest to dominate the surface world."

With this knowledge in hand, the monsters set about preparing for their next move. Little did the Elvians and Wyvinites know the greatest threat to their existence was now lurking in the shadows, waiting to strike.

Chapter 17

The Mountaineers Hunting Trip Gone Awry

Maldreg, Reibeala, and Gulag set out early in the morning, with the sun just starting to peek over the mountain tops. Maldreg was the best hunter in the Mountaineers, known for his stealth and accuracy, while Reibeala was the best navigator, leading the way with her keen sense of direction.

The group were searching for a stag that had been spotted near the base of the mountain. As they approached, they noticed that the stag was surrounded by a pack of vicious wolves, making the hunt even more challenging. Maldreg carefully readied his bow, and Reibeala whispered instructions to Gulag, this his first hunting trip, he was eager to learn the ways of hunting.

Just as Maldreg released his arrow, the ground beneath their feet began to shake. It was an earthquake, a rare occurrence in these mountains, but one that was known to be very dangerous. Gulag stumbled and fell his leg twisting awkwardly as he hit the ground.

Reibeala and Maldreg rushed to his side, both horrified and relieved that he was still conscious. "Gulag, are you okay?" Reibeala asked, her voice tight with worry.

Gulag winced as he tried to move his leg. "I think I broke my leg," he said, gritting his teeth against the pain.

Reibeala and Maldreg quickly assessed the situation. They were too far from the healer at home get help immediate help, and the earthquake had made the rocky terrain even more treacherous. "We'll have to make a splint for your leg and carry you back to the village," Reibeala said, already thinking of the best way to improvise a makeshift crutch.

Maldreg concurred, and the two of them worked together to fashion a splint for Gulag's leg and carry him back to the village. It was a long and difficult journey back home, but they finally made it back, exhausted and without food but relieved to be safe.

Gulag was taken to the healer, who determined that his leg was indeed broken. He was given a poultice to help with the pain. The Healer remembered a story his grandfather used to tell him about sealing wounds with a hot piece of metal. He quickly gathered some equipment, heated a metal rod to a high temperature, and applied it to Gulag's wound. The young boy screamed in pain, but the wound was sealed, preventing any further damage or infection.

Despite the accident, Gulag was even more determined to learn the ways of hunting. He knew that he would have to be stronger and more agile than ever before, and he was ready for the challenge.

Chapter 18

Sealing the Wound and Singing for Ore

The earthquake had also caused another problem for the Mountaineers. Most of the ore veins that they relied on for their survival were now destroyed, leaving them with a limited supply of metal. They had to find a way to access new veins quickly, or face the consequences of not having the materials they needed to sustain their community.

Brarmuk the leader of the mountaineers swiftly approached the centre of the room, looked at Kalgoula and said desperately "you know the ancient songs". "The songs were said to bring the ore veins back to the surface".

With nothing to lose, Kalgoula stood up and started singing an ancient song, gradually followed by all the Mountaineers, their voices echoing through the mountains.

"In the depths of the earth, where the fire meets the stone,
The veins of metal run, with power all their own.
But when disaster strikes, and the earth does shake,
The veins are lost, and their power does fade.
Oh ore veins, hear my call,
Rise up from the earth, and be strong once more.
With every note I sing, may your magic take flight,
And bring forth the metal, to keep us shining bright.
With each word, I sing to you,
My voice, like the wind, will carry it through.
To the depths of the earth, where the fire meets the stone,
And the veins of metal will be restored.
Oh ore veins, hear my call,
Rise up from the earth, and be strong once more.
With every note I sing, may your magic take flight,
And bring forth the metal, to keep us shining bright.
The power takes hold, the ore veins are strong, and the metal shines bold.
We sing this beautiful song,
So that the power of the ore, will live on"

Seconds pass and there's no change. But slowly, they could feel the energy of the earth changing, and the vein of ore they sought began to reveal itself. The Mountaineers all cheers with joy and excitement. For the rest of the day they worked tirelessly to extract it, grateful for the power of their ancestors' songs.

By the end of the day, they had successfully retrieved a significant amount of ore, enough to supply their community for the foreseeable future. They were proud of their accomplishments and grateful for the ancient songs that had helped them through their hour of need.

Chapter 19

Cutter's Concern

Cutter was an Elvian lumberjack who was tired of cutting down trees. He knew that the trees were the reason they were alive and thriving, and he didn't want to be the one responsible for their downfall. He gathered his two closest friends, Albwin and Alvin, and shared his concerns with them.

"We can't keep cutting down these trees," Cutter said. "Soon, we'll have no more left and we'll be in trouble."

Albwin frowned. "Cutter, don't even think about it. We need to keep cutting down the trees to survive. It's the only way."

But Alvin had a different opinion. "I think Cutter's right," he said. "We need to look for other resources. We can't just rely on these trees forever."

Just then, Keijo walked by. She was an Elvian who was always curious and always aware of her surroundings. She noticed the three of them were standing close together, talking in hushed tones, and it seemed suspicious to her.

"What are you guys talking about?" Keijo asked.

The three of them looked at each other, and then looked back at Keijo. "Nothing," Cutter said, shrugging his shoulders.

Keijo raised an eyebrow. "Really? It didn't look like nothing."

But Cutter and his friends stuck to their story. "It's nothing, Keijo," Alvin said. "Just some guy talk."

Keijo smiled, but she wasn't convinced. She had a feeling that Cutter and his friends were up to something. She decided to keep an eye on them, just in case.

"Okay," Keijo said, before walking away. "Just remember, if you need any help, I'm here."

Cutter watched Keijo walk away, feeling grateful for her kindness, but also feeling a little uneasy. He knew that his plan to find other resources was risky, but he also knew that it was almost necessary. He just had to figure out how to make it happen.

Chapter 20

A Rare Find

The earthquake that had hit Cravmod was unlike any other that most of the Mountaineers had ever seen. The ground shook fiercely, causing the mountain to rumble and rocks to tumble down. As the dust cleared, two young boys, Manaec and Araghed, were making their way through the debris.

As they were walking through the debris, they saw the light glistening on the mountain wall. As they stepped closer they realised that they had come across the rarest of diamond lying next to a marking in the wall. Manaec picked the beautiful diamond up "Wow, we could make a fortune selling this!" he said, admiring its shining brilliance. He then pointed to the strange symbol on the wall, "Ha, look, it's a horse," he said with excitement in his voice.

However, Araghed had a different opinion. He peered closely at the marking, squinting his eyes, and then said, "I don't think it's a horse, it looks like Kraken, the legendary monster from the story we heard."

Manaec rolled his eyes, "Come on, Araghed, it's clearly a horse."

Araghed shook his head, "No, no, no. Look at the shape, that's not a tail that's a tentacle, it's exactly like the one from the story of Kraken."

The two boys discussed the marking for a while, their imaginations running wild with the possibilities. They finally decided to take the diamond to Brarmuk, the leader of the Mountaineers. Brarmuk was known for his wise counsel and innovative ideas. They knew that they needed to find out what the diamond would be used for.

As they made their way to find Brarmuk, Manaec and Araghed could feel their excitement growing. They were going to be the ones to make the discovery that would change their village forever.

The young boys finally found Brarmuk. Running to him in excitement

"Brarmuk! Brarmuk! Brarmuk! We found this diamond and a strange marking next to it," said Manaec as they approached the leader.

"It looks like Kraken from the story," added Araghed.

Brarmuk took the diamond from the boys and examined it carefully, turning it over in his hands. "This is indeed a rare find," he said thoughtfully. "I have an idea. What if we give this diamond to Sadeck, the greatest engineer among us? He could use it to create an impenetrable piece of armour, I hope."

"That's a great idea, Brarmuk!" said Manaec, his eyes shining with excitement.

"But we have to be careful," warned Araghed. "No one should know of this, for its safety!"

"Don't worry," said Brarmuk with a smile. "We'll keep it safe, and Sadeck will make sure that it's used for the good of all our people."

And with that, the two boys and Brarmuk set off to find Sadeck, eager to see what he would create with the rare diamond.

Chapter 21

This Is My Home

The sun was shining bright as Nozos, the leader of the Wyvinites, sat on his throne made of dragon bone and stone. He had just finished his morning meetings and was enjoying the peace when Zerig, his son, approached him.

"Father," Zerig asked, "why do we not venture out into new territory? Why do we stay here on these lands, surrounded by the same rocks and stones?"

Nozos frowned. He did not like the suggestion. "We stay here because this is our home, our territory," he said firmly. "We are strong here and do not need to venture out."

Zerig was not satisfied with the answer. "But father, don't you think it would be exciting to explore new lands, to see what is beyond the horizon?"

Nozos grew angrier by the minute. "Insulting our strength is not the way to talk to your leader, I mean father" he said, his voice rising.

Just then, Aetire, one of the young weak looking boys, spoke up nervously. "Maybe we should venture out and start looking. Who knows what we might find?"

Nozos stood up, his eyes blazing with anger. "How dare you suggest such a thing!" he shouted. "Our strength lies in our territory, in our home. We do not need to venture out to prove anything."

Qyvrag, Nozos' right hand man, stepped forward. "I agree with Nozos," he said, backing up his leader. "We are strong here and do not need to venture out into unknown lands."

Zerig backed down, sensing the tension in the room. Nozos sat back down, still angry but now with a sense of satisfaction. The Wyvinites were strong, they did not need to venture out into unknown lands to prove it. They were content with their home and their territory, surrounded by the mountains and their crops.

Chapter 22

The Drought

Cutter was standing outside of his home in the Elvian village, staring up at the sky. The sun was beating down on him mercilessly, and he could feel the heat radiating off the ground. He had never felt anything like this before, not even in the hottest months of the year. He looked around at the other Elvians, and he could see that they were all suffering just like he was.

Weeks had now passed, and there had been no rain, not even any sign of it. The once beautiful tropical days had turned into a dry and hot nightmare. The Elvian's source of food was getting smaller and smaller. The water was on rations, everything was drying up. The little fruits on the trees were wilting, and the trees were starting to look sickly.

Cutter knew that something had to be done, and he was the one to do it. He went to his friends, Albwin and Alvin, and told them about his idea.

"We've been cutting down the trees for too long," said Cutter. "I think that's what's causing the drought!"

Albwin and Alvin both looked at him sceptically, but Cutter persisted. "We need to go to Bari, the magic Elvian, and use the book of magic to make it rain."

At first, Albwin and Alvin were hesitant. But as the days passed and the drought worsened, they agreed to go with Cutter to see Bari. They made their way to Bari's small and secluded home and found her sitting in her home, surrounded by books and candles. She was engrossed in her studies and barely looked up when they entered.

"Bari," said Cutter franticly, "we need your help. There's a drought, and we think it might be because we've been cutting down too many trees."

Bari approved, and her eyes lit up. "I see," she said. "I think I know what to do."

She led the three Elvians to Alberad the leader of the Elvians to tell of her plan. Bari stood before Alberad, with the book of magic in hand. "My lord, I come to ask for your permission to use the magic in this book to help us with the drought," Bari said.

Alberad frowned. "The use of magic is not taken lightly, Bari. What exactly do you propose to do?"

"I believe I can use the magic to bring a little rain to help our trees," Bari explained. "The tree of life is suffering, and we must act quickly to save it."

Alberad was silent for a moment, considering Bari's request. "I understand your concern for our trees, but the use of magic is not without risks. Are you sure that this is the only way?"

"I believe it is, my lord," Bari said, nodding. "The drought is severe, and we need to act fast. I am confident in my abilities, and I promise to use the magic with caution."

Alberad sighed. "Very well, I will give you my permission. But remember, if anything goes wrong, the responsibility falls on you."

"Thank you, my lord," Bari said, bowing before Alberad. "I will try not disappoint you."

With that, Bari turned and left the room, ready to use the magic in the book to bring a little rain and save the tree of life.

Bari and the three Elvian boys made their way to the Tree of Life, a massive tree that was said to be the source of all life in Earnoche. As they made their way to the Tree of Life, word had spread. The entire forest of Elvians were nervously watching on from afar, not knowing what was going to happen.

Bari stepped forward, closed her eyes, opened the book of magic, raised her hand and began to chant an ancient spell.

"By the winds of the north, by the streams of the south
By the light of the moon, and the power of the drought
Bring us now, sweet rain from the sky above
Quench the thirst of the land, bring forth life and love"

As Bari speaks the spell, she focuses all of her energy and intention into bringing forth the desired outcome. The other Elvians stand in silence, holding hands and offering their support to the magic. Slowly, in the distance some clouds begin to gather. They glide over the forest ever so slowly. The first drops of rain begin to fall, bringing relief and joy to all who witness it.

Tiny drops of rain kept falling from the sky, followed by more and more. Soon, the sky was filled with a gentle rain that refreshed the tree of life and all the other trees in the village.

The Elvians cheered as the rain continued to fall, and they knew that they had saved their village. Bari closed the book of magic and smiled.

"I'm glad I could help," she shouted to all. "But remember, we must be careful with the trees. We must use them wisely, or we may find ourselves in this predicament again."

The Elvians assented, grateful for Bari's guidance. They left the tree of life, knowing that they had to be more careful from now on. The drought was over, but they knew that they would have to work together to keep their village healthy and thriving.

Alberad stood on the highest peak of the Elvian forest, surveying the land below. He had been uneasy since the spell Bari had cast to bring rain to the parched earth. He knew that ancient magic was powerful, but he also knew that it came with consequences.

Days had passed since the spell was cast, and Alberad noticed things in the distance, in the forests shadows. He saw what looked like strange lizards lurking in the shadows, and he felt that whatever they were, they were not to be trusted. He felt as if he was being watched.

Chapter 23

Brarmuk's Dilemma

Brarmuk had noticed that the number of Mountaineers was increasing rapidly, and the resources were getting scarce. The water was running low, the systems they had created were not producing enough water and there was not enough room for everyone in the mountains. He was worried about the future of the mountaineers. He thought about leaving the mountains and exploring other lands to find a better place to live or better things to help them live.

One day, while he was walking through the mountain tunnels, he stumbled upon Gobulir. Gobulir was known to be the grumpiest mountaineer, always looking at the negative side of things. Brarmuk thought it would be best to get his opinion on the matter.

"Gobulir, what do you think about the situation? There's not enough room or water for everyone in the mountains, we can't stay here much longer can we? I think we should explore other lands!?" Brarmuk asked.

Gobulir took a deep breath and replied in his usual negative tone, "A lot of Mountaineers will die. It's inevitable. We are simply too many and not enough resources to sustain us all. But this is our home!"

Brarmuk was taken aback by Gobulir's response, but he didn't give up hope. He sought out Norakor and Maldreg, two of the most respected mountaineers in the community, to ask for their opinion. Brarmuk found Norakor first in his dark chamber and asked him the same question "There's not enough room or water for everyone in the mountains, we can't stay here much longer can we? I think we should explore other lands!?" Norakor, being the wise one, replied, "I understand your concerns, Brarmuk. But I believe that it is our duty to find a way to survive, even if it means venturing into unknown lands." At this point Maldreg, the best hunter of the race, overheard the conversation in passing. Maldreg entered the chamber nodding in agreement, and said confidently "We are strong and capable, Brarmuk. We have survived in these mountains for generations. I have faith that we can survive anywhere."

Brarmuk felt encouraged by Norakor and Maldreg's positive outlook, but he still wondered if it was worth the risk. The decision was not an easy one, but Brarmuk knew that something had to be done before it was too late.

He thought about it for a moment and then decided that it was not going to happen. He was not going to sit and watch his people die. He was going to do something about it.

"I won't let that happen. We will venture out and explore the land, find a better place for us to live and things to help us survive," Brarmuk declared to both Norakor and Maldreg, with determination in his voice.

Gobulir secretly followed Brarmuk to Norakor's chamber. At the point of Brarmuk finishing his conversation Gobulir chuckled loudly whilst peering around the doorway, "Good luck with that! The dessert land surrounding us is harshness that no one has ever survived from when going on an expedition. You will be wasting your time!"

But Brarmuk was determined. He had made up his mind, and nothing was going to stop the mountaineers. He knew the journey was going to be tough and maybe impossible, but he was willing to do whatever it takes to ensure the survival of his people, the Mountaineers.

Brarmuk began to make preparations for the journey. From the start of his planning there were problems. To get over these problems he would need to go and speak to Sadeck, he knew he was the only one that could best help them with these obstacles that were in the way of the Mountaineers future.

Brarmuk made his way briskly, time was ticking. Brarmuk walked and stood in front of the large forge where Sadeck was working. The sound of metal being hit echoed through the mountain air. Brarmuk approached Sadeck, "Good day Sadeck, I have come to seek your expertise."

Sadeck looked up from his work, his face covered in soot. "What can I help you with, Brarmuk?"

"I've been thinking about the overpopulation in the mountains and I believe it's time for us to venture out and explore new lands. There are problems getting in our way though. The first problem is the harsh desert that separates us from other potential territories. I was hoping you could come up with a plan to create some sort of heat proof protection clothing for us to cross the desert."

Sadeck rubbed his chin thoughtfully. "I've been thinking about this for some time now, maybe even years. I believe I can create a type of armour that would protect us from the heat, but it would be a challenging task."

Brarmuk's eyes lit up with excitement. "Can you do it, Sadeck? Can you create this armour?"

Sadeck responded. "I can, but it will take time and resources. We'll need to gather the right materials and I'll need to test it to make sure it's durable enough."

Brarmuk nodded. "I understand. Thanks to our ancient song we have the resources and if you need anything else I'll do whatever it takes to help you. We need to find a solution to the overpopulation and this could be our chance to do something about it."

Sadeck clapped Brarmuk on the shoulder. "Let's do this. It's time for the mountaineers to venture out and explore new lands."

Brarmuk stood in awe as he watched and listened to Sadeck talk about the heat proof protection clothing. The engineer was a true genius, always thinking of the next problem to solve. Sadeck stopped in his tracks.

"Brarmuk," Sadeck said, "We've been thinking about the heat, but what about water? What if we run into a sea or an ocean!?"

Brarmuk stopped smiling at this point and turned to Sadeck. "You're right," he said. "I hadn't thought about that". Sadeck instantly replied "But I have an idea. What if we make an underwater device? It could help us breathe and move underwater."

Brarmuk approved. "I like the sound of that. Let's do it."

Sadeck went back to work, his mind racing with ideas. Brarmuk watched as the engineer started to work, his eyes focused on the task at hand.

Sadeck, muttering under his breath "It's simple," "The device takes in air from the surface and converts it into oxygen, which you can breathe underwater. It also has a propulsion system, so you can move through the water."

Brarmuk was impressed. "Sadeck, you're a genius," he said. "This will be a huge help on our journey."

Sadeck embarrassed, not realising Brarmuk could hear what he was saying, smiled. "I'm glad you think so," he said. "I just hope it works."

Brarmuk patted Sadeck on the back. "I have no doubt that it will," he said. "But before you go any further, we need to put this to a vote"

Brarmuk stood before the group of mountaineers, his friends and advisors. They were gathered in the central hall, the largest room in the mountain, to hear what Brarmuk had to say.

"Friends, we are faced with a dilemma. Our land is becoming more and more crowded and resources will become scarce. It is time for us to consider leaving and exploring other lands or stay and find a way to deal with the issue," Brarmuk began.

Sadeck, Maldreg, Norakor, Dugruck, Gobulir, Reibeala and Kalgoula all listened intently. Brarmuk continued, "I've asked Sadeck to come up with a plan for us to be able to safely travel across the harsh desert and even underwater. But before we can proceed, I need to know what you all think. Should we leave the safety of the mountain and venture out into the unknown?"

The room was silent for a moment as the mountaineers considered Brarmuk's proposal. Then, one by one, they voiced their opinions and voted.

"I say we go," said Maldreg confidently.

Norakor indicated his agreement, "I think it's worth a shot. We can't just stay here and hope for the best."

Dugruck, who was known for his level-headedness, weighed in, "I think we need to be cautious. We don't want to put our lives in danger, I vote we stay."

Reibeala, who was always the voice of reason, spoke up next, "I agree with Dugruck. We should think this through carefully we're not prepared for any obstacles we may face."

Gobulir, as usual, negatively said, "I say we stay. We don't know what's out there and I don't want to risk our lives for something uncertain."

Kalgoula, who was usually quiet, surprised everyone by not casting a vote. When asked why, she simply replied, "I don't know. I could not possibly put the fate of the Mountaineers in my hands."

The vote was close, with two mountaineers in favour of leaving, three against it and one not voting. Brarmuk looked around the room, taking in the opinions of his friends and advisors. He knew this was not an easy decision to make. With great thought running through his mind Brarmuk proceeded

"Alright, I understand your worries and concerns. That's two votes for and three votes against leaving. I myself vote we leave. That brings it to a tie breaker. Sadeck, your vote?"

Sadeck, nervously lifting his head from the ground and scanning the room, cleared his throat and said "It is unknown what is out there but we are brave Mountaineers, I vote we leave!"

Brarmuk stood up, in a loud voice said, "It is final, we make our preparations to leave." Looking at Sadeck now, Brarmuk said with optimism and slight scepticism "Sadeck, you know what to do"

As the mountaineers filed out of the room, Brarmuk couldn't help but feel a sense a mixture of uncertainty and hope.

Chapter 24

The Plan and Attack

The lizard monsters slinked back to the shadows where T'kal awaited, a towering beast with scales as black as the night sky. Their scout report was not good news, and they knew that their leader would not be pleased.

"Report," T'kal growled, his red eyes glowing with an intense inner fire.

"Th.. Th.. The Wyvinites," one of the scouts stammered, "they are a formidable force. Their leader, Nozos, is big and powerful beyond measure, and he has a son, Zerig, also strong."

T'kal's eyes narrowed as he considered this information. "And what of their army? How many warriors do they have at their disposal?"

"Their army is not vast, but they're almighty my lord," another scout chimed in. "At least a hundred strong. They are not to be underestimated."

T'kal let out a roar of frustration, causing the ground to shake beneath their feet. "This is unacceptable," he muttered. "We must find a way to defeat them. They cannot be allowed to stand in our way."

The lizard monsters hissed in agreement, knowing that T'kal was always looking for a new challenge, a new conquest. They would not stop until they had achieved their ultimate goal - to rule over all the lands and all the creatures that lived within them.

"We must keep our eyes open," T'kal continued, his voice low and menacing. "We must be ready to strike at a moment's notice. The Wyvinites are our enemies, and we will not rest until they are defeated."

The lizard monsters, under the leadership of their biggest lizard T'kal, had been plotting their surprise attack on the Wyvinites for months. Their scout reports showed that the Wyvinites were strong and fiercely guarded their territory, but T'kal was confident in his army's ability to overcome them. He gathered his top advisors for a final strategy meeting before their approach to Wyvinite.

"We must be cautious as we approach," T'kal warned his advisors. "The Wyvinites are known for their agility and strength. We must take advantage of their weakness and strike when they least expect it."

The advisors all agreed with their leader, and the discussion continued for hours as they fine-tuned their plan. They decided to split their army into smaller groups, each with their own unique strengths, to increase their chances of success. They also discussed the importance of capturing Nozos, the leader of the Wyvinites, alive if possible.

As they neared Wyvinite, the lizard monsters could feel the tension building within their ranks. The Wyvinites had no idea what was about to hit them. T'kal smiled to himself, confident in his army's abilities and the success of their surprise attack.

The approach to Wyvinite was a slow and steady one. The lizard monsters were patient, they had planned their attack for months, and they were determined to make it a successful one. They travelled through the night, careful not to alert the Wyvinites of their presence.

As they approached the edge of the Wyvinite territory, T'kal signalled his troops to prepare for attack. The lizard monsters were well-trained and highly skilled in battle. They had weapons and armour that were designed for maximum protection and strength. T'kal was confident that his army would be able to defeat the Wyvinites.

The first stage of the attack was to create a distraction, so T'kal sent a small group of soldiers to draw the attention of the Wyvinites away from the main army. As they neared the entrance to the Wyvinite territory, T'kal saw Nozos alone but at a distance and had a conversation with him.

"Nozos, hear me," T'kal spoke, his voice booming at Nozos. "Your land is ours now. Surrender and you will be spared."

Nozos was not one to be intimidated, he stood tall and replied, "Never! Wyvinite is ours and we will defend it to our last breath."

T'kal let out a sinister laugh, "Then prepare to meet your doom."

The lizard monsters launched their attack, storming the entrance to Wyvinite. The Wyvinites were caught off guard, but they quickly rallied and fought back with ferocity. Nozos and Zerig, his son, led the charge, the volcanic lava surrounding them blazing bright. T'kal and his army were relentless, and the battle raged on for what seemed like hours.

The clash of weapons echoed through the dark ashy mountains as the two sides battled. Fire rained down as they fought. The ground shook as they collided and the air was filled with the screeches of the lizard monsters and the roars of the Wyvinites. The battle was intense, and it seemed as though it would never end.

Despite their best efforts, the Wyvinites were slowly being pushed back. T'kal and his army were relentless, and they showed no mercy. Nozos and Zerig, looking fatigued and injured, fought on, determined to protect their home and their people. However, it seemed as though all was lost, until Nozos flew high above the clouds stretched out his wings and flung lava from the volcano down onto the lizard monsters.

He had created a new weapon, one that would turn the tide of the battle. The scorching hot lava continued to strike the lizard monsters with tremendous force. The lizard army was taken aback by this, and they began to retreat. Nozos and Zerig took advantage of this and launched a counter-attack, driving the lizard monsters back and forcing them to flee.

The battle was over, and Wyvinite was saved. The Wyvinites emerged victorious, but they had suffered great losses. Nozos and Zerig were wounded, but they were alive. They had defended their home and their people, and they had proven their strength and bravery with the little numbers they had.

The lizard monsters retreated, but they were not defeated. T'kal was furious, he had been so close to victory, but his plans had been thwarted. He would not give up, he would return, and he would take Wyvinite. But for now, the Wyvinites were safe.

Chapter 25

Toru's Solitude

Toru sat on the edge of the pier, watching the waves crash against the shore. He was embarrassed and angry with himself. He couldn't believe he had been caught stealing. He had always prided himself on his stealth and cunning, but this time he had failed. The thought of everyone in town looking down on him was too much to bear.

He stood up and walked along the pier, lost in thought. He was so lost in his thoughts that he didn't even realise that he had walked far out into the ocean, looking back he could barely see home. He looked up and saw the sun setting over the horizon, casting a warm glow over the water.

He muttered to himself, "How could I have been so stupid? I should have known better. Now I'm just a common thief and a liar."

Toru asked himself. "I've already tarnished my reputation. No one will ever trust me again will they?"

The voice in his head chuckled. "You're thinking too small, Toru. You have the potential for greatness. Don't let this setback define you. Use it as motivation to do better."

Toru stopped and looked out over the ocean. The vast expanse of water seemed to go on forever, and it made him feel small and insignificant. His thoughts were interrupted as he started to hear a loud splashing sound. It was getting louder and closer and Toru was starting to feel spooked. He thought about running back to shore but his feet wouldn't move.

"What is that?" Toru muttered to himself as he looked out into the dark waters.

The splashing grew louder and suddenly, Toru saw what looked like a huge tentacle rising from the water in the distance. He couldn't believe his eyes and he backed away from the edge of the pier.

"Is that the Kraken?" Toru whispered to himself, his heart racing.

He watched as the tentacle disappeared back into the water and he let out a sigh of relief. But just as he was about to turn around and go back to shore, he heard the splashing start up again. This time, it was even louder and closer.

"No, this can't be happening," Toru said as he backed away further.

Toru screamed and started to run back to shore. He didn't look back and just ran as fast as he could. He didn't stop until he was back in the centre of Postis and he was panting and sweating. He had never been so scared in his life.

As Toru stumbled back, gasping for air and shaking with fear. Triton, Roka, and Nixie were the first to greet him, with looks of concern etched on their faces.

"Toru, what's the matter?" asked Triton, his voice steady and commanding.

"I saw it! I swear! I saw Kraken!" exclaimed Toru, his voice trembling with fear.

Nixie rolled her eyes and shouted, "Oh come on, not this again! Toru always lies about seeing the most absurd creatures. It's just an excuse for him to get attention."

Roka spoke up. "That's impossible, Toru. We've lived in these waters for many years now, and we've never seen Kraken. It's just a myth, passed down from generation to generation."

Triton's face darkened with anger. "Toru, if you're lying about this, it's not a joke. It's dangerous to spread false information."

But Toru was insistent. "I'm not lying, I swear! I saw it with my own eyes! It was huge, with tentacles and a massive mouth!"

Triton sighed, shaking his head. "Go back home, Toru. We'll deal with this later. I don't want to hear any more of your tales."

Toru hung his head as he made his way back home, feeling embarrassed and angry once again. He had only wanted to help the others. As he made his way home, he couldn't help but wonder if he had actually seen Kraken.

Chapter 26

Vision of the Monster

It was a beautiful spring day in Earnoche, the children were playing and you could hear their laughter throughout the forest. The Elvians were going about their day to day activities including Bari. Bari always walked through the forest in the morning as she felt more connected to nature at this time. She walked slowly towards the Tree of Life, her hand outstretched towards its rough bark, as she does every morning. As she placed her hand on the tree, she felt a sudden jolt of energy run through her. The energy was overwhelming, and she saw visions of a monster that she had never seen before.

"Alberad! Cutter! Elegast! Keijo!" she called out to her fellow Elvians as she stumbled away from the Tree of Life.

The four Elvians came running over to see what was wrong. "What is it, Bari?" Alberad asked, concern engraved on his face.

"I.. I.. I had a vision of a monster," Bari said, her voice shaking. "It was unlike anything I've ever seen before. I think it might have been..... Kraken."

"Kraken?" Keijo exclaimed. "But that's just a myth. Kraken isn't real."

"It felt real to me," Barked Bari. "And I've never had a vision like this before."

"We need to call a proper meeting to discuss this in private," Elegast said. "We need to figure out what to do if this monster is real."

Alberad summoned his council of leaders to a meeting, the five Elvians gathered at the great hall and they discussed what could be done to protect their people. "If this monster is real," Alberad said. "And if it is, we need to find a way to help ourselves."

"But how?" Cutter asked. "How do we even start to help ourselves?"

"We can also check the ancient texts," Elegast added. "There might be something there that can give us a clue about what our next move should be."

Alberad without hesitation bellowed "We are not using The Book of Magic again Elegast!"

There was a moment of silence in the hall, you could hear a pin drop.

Alberad continued with little patience "I suggest that we should venture out into the unknown lands, searching for a new home where we could start anew or find something that can protect us without consequence." Some of them were hesitant, but Alberad was determined to find a solution.

"We need to act fast," Alberad said. "If this monster is real and it's coming for us, we need to be ready."

The Elvians responded with agreement, and the meeting was finished. They knew that they needed to work together to find out the truth about the monster and protect their home or find a new one. For the sake of their people, they hoped that their journey would lead to a brighter future.

Chapter 27

Mountaineers Preparation and Execution

Brarmuk made his way over to Sadeck's workshop, eager to see the progress of the heat proof clothing and underwater gear. He pushed open the door and called out to Sadeck, "How's it going? Have you finished the heat proof clothing and underwater gear yet?"

Sadeck looked up from his workbench and dipped his head, "Almost there, Brarmuk. I'll have it ready in an hour, just need to make a few final adjustments."

"Good work," Brarmuk said, clapping Sadeck on the back. "Meet me in the hall in an hour with everything, we need to be prepared for anything on our journey."

Sadeck nodded, "Will do. I just hope these work as well as we need them to."

Brarmuk replied, "We have to have faith, Sadeck. The mountaineers are counting on us to find a solution to our problems. And these pieces of gear may just be the answer we're looking for."

Sadeck replied, "I understand. I'll make sure everything is ready in an hour."

Brarmuk smiled and left the workshop, feeling confident that the gear would be ready in time. He made his way back to the hall to gather the rest of the team and prepare for their journey.

Brarmuk made his way to the hall with authority, where Maldreg, Dugruck, Gobulir, and Reibeala were already gathered. They all turned to face him as he approached.

"We're leaving in an hour," Brarmuk announced. "I need all of you to gather food, water, and weapons for our journey. Sadeck will have the heat proof clothing and underwater gear ready by then."

"Underwater gear?" Gobulir asked, a hint of scepticism in his voice.

"Yes, just in case we come across any bodies of water in or after the harsh dessert," Brarmuk explained.

"I'll gather the food," Maldreg said.

"I'll get the water," Dugruck added.

"I'll take care of the weapons," Gobulir grumbled.

"And I'll help with whatever is needed," Reibeala said, eager to assist.

"Good," Brarmuk said, pleased with their quick response. "We need to be well prepared for this journey. The consequences of not being prepared could be dire. Reibeala please gather two more of the strongest and fastest Mountaineers you know, they will leave with you"

The four mountaineers quickly set to work, each taking on their assigned task with determination. Brarmuk watched them for a moment before turning to leave the hall.

"I'll meet you all back here in an hour," he said over his shoulder as he left.

The group worked efficiently, each of them determined to make sure their expedition was as well-equipped as possible. As the hour passed, they regathered in the hall, each of them with a full pack on their back.

"Alright," Brarmuk said, looking them over. "Are we all ready?"

"Yes," they answered in unison.

"Good," Brarmuk said. "You all better get going."

"What!?" Gobulir moaned loudly "you're not coming!?"

"No, I need to stay here and look after things here in Cravmod," Brarmuk said. "You all better get going, good luck"

"We're going to need it" Sadeck and Gobulir said under their breathe at the same time.

With that, the group set out, ready to embark on their journey into the unknown. The consequences of their actions weighed heavily on them, but they were determined to succeed, no matter what lay ahead.

Sadeck, Maldreg, Dugruck, Gobulir, Reibeala and a couple other Mountaineers had their newly created heat proof clothing, ready for their journey through the desert that started at the base of the mountain. The sun was blazing hot, and the air was dry and suffocating.

"Alright everyone, let's put on our heat proof clothing," Sadeck instructed as they took their first steps into the scorching desert.

They had been walking through the desert for two days now. Their food and water supplies were dwindling.

As they woke up on their third day of travelling they continued walking, their goal the only thing motivating them. As they walked, Maldreg took on the responsibility of hunting for food. With their supplies running low, Maldreg was tasked with finding a source of sustenance to keep them sustained on their journey.

Reibeala, who was a skilled navigator, was leading the way through the desert. She had spent time studying maps and the geography of the area, and was confident that she knew the best route to take if there was an end to this treacherous desert.

"We've been walking for days, and I'm getting tired," Gobulir complained.

"We can't stop now, we have to keep moving forward," Maldreg replied.

"But I'm hungry," Gobulir added.

"I'll see if I can find anything," Maldreg offered, "I'll keep my eyes peeled."

"Thanks Maldreg, we all appreciate your help," Dugruck said.

As they continued to travel, they encountered many challenges, including scorching sand storms, and the relentless heat. But they pressed on, determined to reach their destination.

"We're running low on water, we need to find a source soon," Sadeck said.

"Reibeala, will there be any oasis nearby?" Maldreg asked.

Reibeala knelt to the floor, waving her hands in the sand and pulling up a hand full of sand, she raised her hand and released the sand, the harsh winds blowing it away. Looking at Maldreg with sorrowful eyes but only so he could see.

"There's one a few miles ahead, we should reach it by nightfall," Reibeala replied.

The hours passed and darkness had almost taken over.

"We're making good progress, let's get some rest and start again in the morning," Maldreg said as they settled in for the night. All so exhausted they had forgotten Reibeala's words.

The morning sun had risen and despite the challenges they faced, the group remained determined and continued on their journey, one step at a time.

As the group of Mountaineers continued their journey through the harsh desert, the heat was beaming down on them. Suddenly, Dugruk let out a loud scream "Arrrrrggghhhhh" and stumbled forward, clutching at his chest. The group rushed to his side, quickly realising that his heat proof clothing had failed.

"What happened?" Maldreg asked, concern chiselled on his face.

"My heat proof clothing broke, there's a hole," Dugruk answered, panting heavily. "I can't handle this heat anymore."

Sadeck quickly fell to his knees to inspect the damaged clothing, his brow furrowed in concentration. "It's beyond repair," he announced after a few moments. "I don't have the equipment or materials to fix it here."

"What do we do now?" Gobulir asked, worry in his voice.

"He needs to go back," Maldreg said firmly. "We'll send him back with the two mountaineers we brought with us. We can't afford to lose any more members on this journey."

Dugruk shook, looking disappointed. "I'll try and make it back."

"Be careful, go the way we came," Reibeala said, clasping on the shoulder of Dugruk.

"We will," Dugruk said gasping for air, before turning to make his way back, accompanied by the two mountaineers.

The remaining members of the group continued on, but the mood was somber. They all knew the dangers that lay ahead and the fact that they were losing members was not a good sign. But they also knew that they had to keep moving forward, no matter what obstacles lay in their way.

"We'll make it through this," Maldreg said, breaking the silence. "We'll find what we're looking for and make it back home safe and sound."

The others acknowledged and agreed, determination in their eyes. They continued on, with Reibeala navigating the way.

As the sun began to set, Reibeala screeched "look over there at the horizon, is that….is that water!?"

As the group of travellers got closer they could see it was the ocean, they could see the vast expanse of water stretching out before them. The sight of it after days of trekking through the hot desert was a welcome relief. They all broke out into laughter and cheers.

"We made it!" Maldreg exclaimed as he ran towards the shore.

"Finally, some fresh water," Reibeala added, following close behind.

The group gathered around the edge of the water, eager to drink and replenish themselves. Gobulir turned to Sadeck, who had brought a water purifier with him. "Sadeck, can you get us some water?"

"Of course, it's what I brought the purifier for," Sadeck replied, setting up the device.

"Thank the gods for Sadeck and his inventions," Gobulir said, taking a long drink of the purified water.

"Yeah, this is a lifesaver," Maldreg added, wiping the water from his chin.

The group spent the next hour drinking and replenishing themselves. They discussed their plans for the next stage of their journey, now that they had reached the ocean. They were all in high spirits, grateful for the break from the harsh desert.

"We've come a long way," Maldreg said, looking out over the water. "But we still have a long way to go. Let's make the most of this moment and get some rest, then we'll set off again tomorrow morning."

The group nodded in unity and settled in for a well-deserved rest by the ocean. Their conversations and laughter echoed across the shore as they took a break from their journey and enjoyed the moment of peace.

The sun rose high in the sky and Reibeala, Sadeck, Maldreg and Gobulir finally reached the ocean they had been dreaming of. They were all excited to see what was under the water, but also a bit nervous about using the underwater gear that Sadeck had brought with them.

As soon as the crystal clear waters hit their toes, Sadeck handed each of them a diving suit. Gobulir was hesitant at first, eyeing the gear with suspicion.

"What is this?" Gobulir asked, picking up the bulky suit. "I don't trust this thing. It looks dangerous."

Sadeck chuckled. "It's not dangerous, I promise. It's a diving suit. It will allow us to breathe underwater and protect us from the pressure."

"How does it work?" Gobulir asked, still looking uncertain.

"The diving suit has a built-in air tank that provides us with air while we are underwater. The goggles will allow us to see clearly underwater," Sadeck explained, putting on his own suit.

Reibeala, Maldreg, and Gobulir followed Sadeck's lead, and soon they were all suited up and ready to go. They stepped into the water, and as soon as their heads were underwater, they could feel the weight of the gear on their bodies. But the feeling soon faded as they marvelled at the beauty of the underwater world.

"Wow," Reibeala breathed, looking around in wonder. "I've never seen anything like this."

"It's incredible," Maldreg added, his voice muffled by the diving suit.

Sadeck led the way, pointing out different species of fish and plants as they explored the underwater world. Gobulir, who had been hesitant at first, was now in awe of the beauty around him.

"I never knew the world could be this beautiful," Gobulir said, his voice filled with wonder.

They swam for hours, taking in all the sights and sounds of the underwater world.

Reibeala, Sadeck, Maldreg and Gobulir finally made it to the bottom of the ocean. They were amazed at the vast array of creatures that swam around them and marvelled at the beauty of the underwater landscape. Sadeck was particularly impressed with the vibrant coral and diverse marine life.

The amazement was soon halted by Maldreg. After a while, he began to feel like something was watching them. "Guys, I think we're being watched," Maldreg whispered to the group. The others looked around, but saw nothing.

"What do you mean, Maldreg?" Reibeala asked, her voice filled with concern.

"I don't know. I just feel like there's something here, watching us," Maldreg replied, looking around nervously.

Gobulir and Reibeala shared Maldreg's concerns and they all began to feel uneasy. As Maldreg was the Mountaineers best hunter and nothing usually fazed Maldreg.

Suddenly, Gobulir was bumped into by something big and strong and it swam away without being seen. They all panicked, not knowing what it was. They started running away across the ocean floor as fast as they could, their hearts pounding in their chest.

"What was that?" Gobulir shouted, his voice filled with fear.

"I don't know, but let's get out of here," Reibeala replied, leading the way.

After a few minutes of running, they finally found some land. They all breathed a sigh of relief and looked around. They saw nothing out of the ordinary, but they all still felt on edge. They decided to stick together and keep a close eye on each other, just in case.

Chapter 28

Toru felt terrible after everything that had happened recently. He had been caught stealing and was met with anger and embarrassment from Triton and the others. In an effort to make himself feel better, he went to see Nixie and Ari.

"Hey guys," Toru said, approaching the two of them. "Triton has asked me to gather some gems out in the ocean, and I was wondering if you'd like to come with me."

Nixie looked sceptical. "Really? I thought Triton was still upset with you," she said.

Ari indicated his agreement. "Yeah, I'm not sure if he would have asked you to do something like that."

Toru tried to wave their concerns away. "Oh, it's fine. He's over it now. And besides, I could use some company out there."

Nixie and Ari looked at each other, and then back at Toru. "Well, I guess it wouldn't hurt to go with you," Nixie said.

Ari responded. "Yeah, let's do it. It'll be an adventure."

So the three of them set off towards the ocean, eager to explore and find some gems along the way. As they travelled, Toru couldn't help but feel a sense of excitement. He was determined to make the most of this opportunity and forget about his recent troubles.

As they reached the water's edge, they dove into the ocean. Toru led the way, swimming towards a nearby reef that he had heard was full of valuable gems. Nixie and Ari followed close behind, and the three of them explored the reef together, marvelling at the stunning coral and the various sea creatures that surrounded them.

As they swam, Toru couldn't help but feel a sense of joy and freedom. He was surrounded by the beauty of the ocean, and he felt like he was finally able to escape his recent troubles.

Toru, Nixie, and Ari made their way out further and further in the ocean and they heard rushing water. The three of them looked and saw a big rock. They made their way over to the rock and as they stood there they realised they were on the edge of a dangerous waterfall, peering down into the rushing waters below. The sound of the waterfall echoed through the air as they looked out into the distance.

Suddenly, Toru pointed down below in the distance "look" they could see figures in the water. "They seem to be diving into it, one after the other." Exclaimed Ari.

"What do you think they're doing?" Nixie asked, her voice filled with curiosity.

"They must be searching for something," Toru replied.

"I hope they know what they're doing," Ari added.

"Come on, let's go see what they're up to," Toru said, starting to make his way down the waterfall.

Nixie hesitated. She had never been a fan of heights, and the thought of climbing down the waterfall made her stomach turn. "I don't think this is a good idea, Toru. We should go back."

"Don't be scared, Nixie," Toru said, trying to reassure her. "We'll be fine. Ari and I will be here to help you."

Nixie sighed, knowing that she didn't want to be left alone on the top of the waterfall. She reluctantly followed Toru and Ari as they made their way down the waterfall, their feet slipping and sliding on the slippery rocks.

As they reached the bottom of the waterfall, they dived in the water and they saw that the figures they had seen earlier were actually a group of people, dressed in strange bulky gear and walking on the ocean floor. They were searching for something, and Toru, Nixie, and Ari were determined to find out what.

Ari, Nixie and Toru stood at the bottom of the dangerous waterfall, looking down at the group of people in the distance. As they jumped in Ari noticed that the group were very slow to move and that they didn't have good visibility with their big suits. He turned to Toru and said, "They're not moving very fast, and they don't seem to have much visibility. I think we could use that to our advantage."

Toru approved and had a mischievous grin spread across his face. "I've got an idea," he said. "Let's go scare them a little."

Nixie's eyes widened in horror. "We can't do that! It's not nice, and it could be dangerous. We have just found 'other people' for the first time and you want to scare them!?" she said.

"Come on, Nixie," Toru said, rolling his eyes. "It'll be fun. We'll just swim over and make some loud noises. They'll probably just think it's some kind of sea creature. They'll be harmless, they have on swim suits for Christ sakes."

Nixie hesitated, looking back and forth between Ari and Toru. "I don't know," she said. "I don't want to get in trouble with Triton."

"Don't worry, Nixie," Ari said, patting her arm. "It'll be fine. We'll just swim over, make some noise, and then swim back. No one will even know it was us."

Reluctantly, Nixie agreed, and the three of them set off towards the group of people. But Toru suddenly burst forward leaving Ari and Nixie behind.

Toru swam silently and swiftly closer and closer to the group. He stopped and waited until they could not possibly see him. He burst towards them and pushed one with his feet and burst off without being seen. Toru could hear their screams as he swam off.

The group of people were quickly spooked and started running away as fast as they could, clearly terrified. Ari and Nixie tried to stifle their laughter as they watched Toru's little trick play out.

As they swam back to the waterfall, Nixie couldn't help but feel a little guilty about what they had just done. She knew it wasn't very nice, but she couldn't deny that it had been fun. "Toru that was uncalled for and not very nice!" she said but laughed as soon as she finished speaking.

Toru, on the other hand, was feeling quite pleased with himself. He had never been one to follow the rules, and he loved nothing more than a good prank. He was already thinking of what other pranks he could pull on their next adventure.

Toru, Nixie, and Ari made their way back to Postis, ensuring they were careful when climbing the waterfall again. They were excited to share their story with Triton and Zale. As they approached the main coral hall, Toru took a deep breath, ready to face Triton's scepticism.

"We have something to tell you," Toru announced as they entered the hall.

Triton raised an eyebrow, his scepticism evident. "What is it now, Toru?"

"We went out exploring….quite far out in the ocean and we found some other people," Toru said, trying to sound confident.

Nixie and Ari were united in their understanding, adding their own accounts of the experience. "Yes, they were at the bottom of the ocean and seemed to be struggling with the lack of visibility," Ari said.

Triton was still sceptical. "And you expect me to believe this?" he asked, crossing his arms.

"It's true!" Nixie interjected. "We saw it with our own eyes."

Zale looked at Triton, sensing the tension. "Let's hear them out," he suggested.

Triton sighed, relenting. "Fine, go on," he said.

Toru continued, describing the figures in the distance and the realisation that they were slow to move. He explained how he had come up with the idea to scare the group, much to Nixie's dismay.

"I know it was a silly idea, but it worked," Toru said, shrugging.

Nixie and Ari nodded in agreement, eager to defend their friend. "It was a harmless prank," Ari said.

Triton sighed, rubbing his temples. "I don't know what to make of this," he said. "If this is true you can take Zale and I back to see them for ourselves then?"

Toru, Nixie, and Ari beamed with excitement, grateful for the chance to continue their exploration. "Yes that's right" Toru Said. Ari Pipped up as well "of course we can" Nixie stepped forward and looked at Triton and said "I wouldn't lie to you Triton".

As Ari, Nixie and Toru led Triton and Zale towards the waterfall, Triton grew increasingly agitated. It was taking a while and he couldn't help but think they were lying. When they finally reached the waterfall and got to the edge and looked down at the raging water below, Triton's anger boiled over.

"What were you thinking?! This is incredibly dangerous! You shouldn't have come here, let alone brought us along," he scolded.

Zale agreed, adding, "This is not a safe place for any of us, especially not for young ones like you."

Toru tried to explain that they had seen something at the bottom of the waterfall and wanted to show it to Triton and Zale, but Triton wasn't having any of it.

"We can't risk our safety for something that may not even be real. I think it's best if you all go back home and stay there, immediately," Triton said firmly.

Nixie, Toru and Ari looked at each other, all feeling a mix of disappointment and fear. They had wanted to show Triton and Zale what they had discovered, but now it seemed that their efforts would be for nothing.

As they started to make their way back home, Toru couldn't help but feel a twinge of resentment towards Triton. He thought that they were old enough to make their own decisions and that they should be trusted.

Despite his frustration, Toru knew that Triton only had their safety in mind and that it was best to follow his instructions.

Triton and Zale sat on top of the rock, gazing out at the vast expanse of the ocean. The water from the waterfall was flowing and the sun was shining, casting a warm glow over the entire area.

"Can you believe it?" Triton said, breaking the silence. "No one has ever gone past this point before. We're the first to ever see what lies beyond."

Zale added. "It's incredible to think about all the possibilities. Who knows what we'll find out there?"

Triton looked over at Zale. "Do you ever feel scared about venturing into the unknown?"

Zale shook his head. "Not really. I mean, sure, it can be a bit intimidating. But the excitement of discovery and the potential for new knowledge is what drives me."

Triton smiled. "I feel the same way. I couldn't imagine living a life without exploring and finding new things."

They sat in silence for a few more moments, taking in the beauty of the ocean and thinking about all the adventures yet to come.

"Well, I suppose we should start making our way back," Triton said, finally standing up. "Who knows what we'll find on our next journey."

But as they were about to leave, Triton noticed movement on a bit of land in the distance.

Triton said with curiosity "Zale, do you see that?" he pointed towards the land.

"What is it? Is it just a trick of the light?" Zale said whilst rubbing his eyes.

Triton replied "No, I don't think so. It looks like there's someone or something out there."

Zale still couldn't believe it "That's impossible! We've never seen anyone else in the entire ocean before."

Triton said realising that Toru, Nixie and Ari were not lying "I know, but there it is, right in front of us. We have to go check it out."

"You're right. Let's go see what it is." Exclaimed Zale.

As they approached the land, they couldn't believe their eyes. There were indeed other people out there. They had never seen anything like it before.

Triton quietly turned to Zale "Who are they? And what are they doing here?"

As confused as Triton was, Zale replied "I don't know, but we have to find out. Let's go talk to them."

With excitement and a bit of nervousness, Triton and Zale made their way towards the unfamiliar figures on the distant land. They couldn't wait to find out what they had discovered.

Chapter 29

Meeting the Aquanauts

Triton and Zale emerged from the water, their figures suddenly appearing in front of Maldreg, Reibeala, Sadeck, and Gobulir. The four Mountaineer explorers were caught off guard and stumbled back in surprise, their eyes wide with fear.

"Who are you?" Reibeala asked, her voice shaking.

"We are Triton and Zale," Triton said, his voice calm and reassuring. "We are the guardians of the water world."

"Guardians?" Maldreg repeated, his hand hovering near his weapon.

"Yes," Zale said. "We are the protectors of the ocean and its inhabitants."

Sadeck stepped forward, his curiosity getting the better of him. "What kind of inhabitants?"

"All sorts," Triton said with a smile. "Fish and sea creatures."

Reibeala, Maldreg, Sadeck, and Gobulir exchanged stunned glances. They had never heard of seen other people living anywhere before.

"We've never seen anything like this before," Reibeala said, her eyes taking in the world around them.

"It's a strange and wonderful place," Zale agreed.

Sadeck was eager to learn more. "Can you tell us about it?"

Triton and Zale smiled and welcomed the four explorers back to Postis. They led them through the water landscape, pointing out different creatures and sharing stories about the history of the ocean.

As they walked and swam they talked and asked questions, each of them fascinated by the other. They learned that the water world was a peaceful and harmonious place, where all the creatures lived in harmony.

Maldreg was impressed by the strength and knowledge of the water guardians. "You must be very strong to protect such a vast and dangerous place."

Triton chuckled. "We have been doing it for a very long time and have become quite skilled at it."

Gobulir was amazed. "I have never seen anything like this before. It is truly a wondrous place."

As they continued their journey, Triton and Zale showed them around their home and introduced them to some of the creatures that lived there. They were amazed by the beauty and wonder of the water world and were grateful for the opportunity to experience it.

Maldreg, Reibeala, Sadeck, and Gobulir were awestruck as they stepped onto the land and saw the sparkling jewels of the Aquanauts. Gobulir's eyes were fixated on the gems and he couldn't take his gaze off of them.

"What are these?" Gobulir whispered in wonder.

"These are the jewels of the Aquanauts," Triton replied. "We use them for trade and as currency and they help us."

Gobulir reached out to touch the gems, but Triton stopped him. "Be careful, they are valuable and fragile."

"I've never seen anything like this before," Gobulir said, still in awe.

"These gems are precious and vital to us here in Postis," Zale added. "Beautiful aren't they Gobulir."

Sadeck stepped forward, intrigued. "How do you mine these gems?"

"Yes, how do you mine these" Gobulir interjected.

Triton and Zale exchanged a look. "It's a dangerous process," Triton said. "But it's worth it for the beauty and value of the gems."

Gobulir spoke up, "I would love to see how it's done."

"We can take you to see the mines," Triton said, "but it's not for the faint of heart."

Maldreg stepped forward. "We've taken up enough of their time Gobulir."

Triton Insisted it was ok and so Triton and Zale led the group towards the closest gem reef they knew, their conversation turning towards the process of mining the jewels and the challenges they faced. Gobulir remained fascinated, his eyes still on the gems, and the rest of the group couldn't help but be drawn in by their beauty.

As the group of adventurers stood by the gem reef, surrounded by the glittering jewels, Zale's voice cut through the silence. "You have to be fast," he warned them. "Removing these gems carries a risk. The reef boulders around us can be unstable and may fall at any moment."

Reibeala's eyes widened as she took in the dangers surrounding them. "Are you saying that we're in danger just by being here?" she asked her voice tight with worry.

Triton stepped forward and placed a hand on Reibeala's shoulder. "Zale is just cautioning us," he said, trying to calm her. "As long as we're careful and always aware, we should be okay."

Maldreg acknowledge Triton, his gaze flickering from the gems to the reef boulders towering above them. "We've faced dangers before," he said, his voice resolute. "We can handle this."

Sadeck chimed in, his hands held up in a calming gesture. "Let's just take it slow and steady. We can do this."

Gobulir, who had been entranced by the gems, finally tore his gaze away from them. "I agree," he said, his voice filled with determination. "Shall we see how this is done then?"

The group were in harmony with their agreement, their nerves steeled as they prepared to face the risks of the reef and harvest the valuable gems. They knew that time was of the essence and that they had to work quickly and efficiently if they wanted to succeed. But with a determination that could not be quenched, they set to work, their hands steady as they worked to collect the one precious stone that stood out. A marvellous glistening red stone that was as beautiful as anything they've ever seen. Zale worked away carefully with precision and after what seemed an hour, Zale pulled the gem out and raised it high for all to see.

Everyone was smiling with joy having seen this process and the reward. Zale then placed the gem in Maldreg's hand. "You can take this home." He said. Gobulir had a look of envy on his face, he could not believe he wasn't given the gem.

Eventually, it was time for the four explorers to return to Cravmod. But they knew that they would never forget their encounter with Triton and Zale, the guardians of the water world.

"Thank you for showing us this place," Reibeala said as they began to make their way back.

"It was our pleasure," Triton said with a smile. "And if you ever need our help, just let us know. We will be here."

With a final wave, Triton and Zale disappeared beneath the water, leaving the four explorers to continue their journey, their minds filled with the wonder and magic of the water world.

Chapter 30

Return of the Lizard Monsters

T'kal and the rest of the lizard monsters were returning to their home after their defeat to the Wyvinites. The atmosphere was tense, as T'kal was fuming with anger. His pride had been shattered and he was not happy about the outcome of the battle.

"What happened out there?" T'kal growled as he entered the main chamber of the lair.

"The Wyvinites were too strong for us," one of the lizard monsters replied timidly.

"Too strong? We are the most powerful creatures in this world! How could they have defeated us so easily?" T'kal raged.

The other lizard monsters shuffled their feet nervously, unsure of how to respond to their leader's anger.

"We must regroup and come up with a better strategy," T'kal said after a few moments of silence. "We cannot let this defeat go unanswered."

"But T'kal, we cannot win against them," another lizard monster spoke up. "Their strength is too powerful for us."

T'kal was pacing back and forth, his long tail whipping the air in frustration.

"We cannot let the defeat to the Wyvinites be the end of us," T'kal growled. "We must come up with a plan to reclaim our honour and prove our strength."

The other monsters grumbled in agreement, their eyes gleaming with determination.

"What if we attacked the Elvians?" one of them suggested. "They are a weaker species, and we could easily overpower them."

T'kal considered this for a moment, his sharp claws tapping against the stone floor. "Yes, that could work," he said finally. "The Elvians are known for their beauty and their love of peace. They would never expect an attack from us."

The group of monsters cheered at this, their spirits lifting at the thought of a new battle. T'kal raised his hand for silence.

"But we must be careful," he warned. "The Elvians may not be as weak as they appear. We must gather all of our remaining forces and strike when they least expect it."

The lizard monsters were all approving, their conversations filled with excitement as they began to plan their attack on the unsuspecting Elvians. They were determined to reclaim their place as the strongest species in the land and to make amends for their failure. They knew that T'kal would stop at nothing to avenge their defeat, and they were willing to do whatever it takes to help him achieve his goals.

Chapter 31

Rallying the Troops

T'kal stood before his minions, his eyes scanning the crowd of lizard monsters. He had come up with a plan to distract his troops from their defeat at the hands of the Wyvinites and shift their focus back to the Elvians.

"Listen up, my friends….My family," T'kal began, his voice low and menacing. "We may have lost the battle against the Wyvinites, but we will not be defeated. We will take back what is rightfully ours and conquer the land once again."

The lizard monsters erupted into a frenzy, their roars and hisses filling the air. T'kal raised his hand, signalling for them to calm down.

"We will sneak through the land, avoiding detection by the Elvians. We will make our way to Earnoche, their capital, and strike them where it hurts the most. We will show them that we are not to be underestimated."

T'kal's minions cheered, ready for battle. They set out on their journey, the stealthy footsteps of their troops the only sound that echoed through the land.

As they made their way closer to Earnoche, the lizard monsters were filled with anticipation and excitement. They were ready for the fight that was to come, and T'kal was confident in their abilities to defeat their enemies.

"Stay alert, my minions," T'kal warned as they approached the city gates. "The Elvians will not go down easily. But with our strength and cunning, we will come out victorious."

The lizard monsters nodded, their eyes gleaming with determination. They knew that this was going to be a tough battle, but they were ready to face any challenge that lay ahead of them.

The sun was lying low, the light just peeking through the leaves of the forest. Cutter, Albwin and Alvin were out in the forest, cutting down trees, preparing for the upcoming winter.

As they worked, they felt a strange energy in the air, a sense of unease that they couldn't quite explain.

Meanwhile, Bari was making her way towards the Tree of Life, as she did every morning. Bari was honoured to be able to approach it.

Alberad, meanwhile, was playing with the Elvian children, laughing and joking with them as they ran through the forest.

But little did they know, the lizard monsters were silently making their way through the land, determined to attack the Elvian people. The monsters were filled with rage and hatred, driven by a desire for blood.

As the monsters approached Earnoche, the sense of unease grew stronger. The Elvians had no idea of the danger that was coming their way, but they would soon find out.

As the lizard monsters approached Earnoche, they felt a rush of excitement. They had come up with a plan to attack a few lone Elvians in order to weaken the enemy's defence. They approached the outskirts of the city, hiding behind trees and bushes. They communicated with hand signals, silently making their way forward.

"Remember, we need to be stealthy," T'kal whispered to his troops. "The element of surprise is our biggest advantage."

The monsters slowly crept forward, their eyes fixed on their targets. The lone Elvians were completely unaware of the danger that was approaching them. Suddenly, the monsters pounced, moving with lightning speed. The Elvians were caught off guard, completely caught off guard by the sudden attack.

"Attack! Attack!" T'kal whispered with authority, leading the charge.

The Elvians tried to fight back, but they were no match for the strength and ferocity of the lizard monsters. The monsters overpowered them, quickly overpowering them and leaving them lying on the ground, lifeless.

"I can smell victory!" T'kal mumbled to himself, noticing the Tree of Life just ahead.

"The Elvians are no match for us!" one of the monsters exclaimed.

They had taken the first step in their plan to defeat the Elvians and take control of Earnoche. They continued on, marching through the city with determination, ready for whatever challenges lay ahead.

T'Kal led the charge towards the heart of Earnoche, his army of lizard monsters following close behind. The peaceful sound of laughter and joy was quickly replaced by the clash of swords and the roar of beasts.

"Attack!" T'Kal roared as they approached the centre of the city.

The Elvians were caught off guard, but they quickly rallied and fought back. Alberad was among the first to respond, his battle cry ringing out over the chaos.

"Defend Earnoche! Protect our home!" Alberad shouted as he charged towards T'Kal and his minions.

The lizard monsters were fierce, but the Elvians were determined. They fought with all their might, their swords flashing in the sunlight. T'Kal swung his massive claws, each strike sending an Elvian flying.

"We will not be defeated by these creatures!" Alberad yelled as he ducked under T'Kal's attack and struck back with his sword.

T'Kal was relentless, his eyes blazing with anger. He swung his claws again and again, determined to take down the Elvians and conquer their city.

"Stand strong, my friends!" Alberad called out to his fellow Elvians. "We will not fall to these monsters!"

The battle raged on, with neither side giving up. The lizard monsters fought with all their might, while the Elvians stood their ground and fought back with everything they had. In the end, it was unclear who would emerge victorious. But one thing was certain – this was a battle that would go down in history, remembered for generations to come.

Alberad noticed the commotion coming from the other side of the village and quickly realised that a group of lizard monsters had surrounded a group of Elvian children. He immediately ran towards them, his heart racing with fear and anger. "Stay back!" he yelled, brandishing his sword.

The lizard monsters sneered at Alberad and raised their weapons. "Another Elvian hero to play with," one of them said. "We'll enjoy breaking you."

Alberad didn't let their taunts get to him. He focused on the task at hand and launched himself at the monsters, his sword flashing in the sunlight. He swung and parried, dodging their attacks and striking back with all his might. The lizard monsters were no match for his skill and strength, they lay bloodied and broken, Alberad's focus had never been stronger.

Alberad turned to the children, who were huddled together in fear. "Go!" he said, his voice firm but gentle. "Go and hide! I'll protect you."

The children and ran off with great fear running through their minds, disappearing into the trees. Alberad watched them go, his heart heavy with worry. He knew that the lizard monsters were not done yet, and that T'Kal was still a threat. He turned back to the battle, ready to face whatever lay ahead.

As Alberad fought, he could see T'Kal making his way towards the Tree of Life. "No!" Alberad yelled, running towards T'Kal. "You won't destroy it! I won't let you!"

T'Kal finally reached the Tree of Life. The massive, ancient tree towered over him, its roots twisting around the rocky ground. The sun shone down on its leaves, casting a warm glow on T'Kal's face. He stood there for a moment, admiring its beauty.

T'Kal sneered at the tree and raised his weapon. "Foolish Elvians," he said. "Do you think you can stop me?"

Suddenly, a small Elvian with a weapon appeared in front of T'Kal. He looked down and saw Keijo, standing bravely before him. T'Kal laughed. "You think you can stop me…. with that?" he said, gesturing to Keijo's weapon.

Keijo stood firm. "I may not be much, but I will do everything in my power to protect the Tree of Life."

T'Kal sneered, and then lunged forward, swinging his weapon at Keijo. The Elvian was quick, dodging the attack, but T'Kal was relentless. He swung again and again, until finally he struck Keijo, sending her flying across the clearing.

T'Kal then turned his attention back to the Tree of Life. He raised his weapon and struck it, causing a noticeable wound in the trunk. The tree groaned and swayed, but T'Kal was undeterred. He raised his weapon again, ready to strike a fatal blow.

Just then, a figure appeared from nowhere and jumped on T'Kal's back, causing him to lose his balance. T'Kal roared in frustration, struggling to shake the figure off. It was Cutter, one of the Elvian woodcutters.

"You will not harm the Tree of Life!" Cutter yelled, hanging on for dear life.

T'Kal struggled, trying to throw Cutter off, but the Elvian was too slick. With one final burst of energy, T'Kal stumbled, and then fell to the ground. Cutter jumped off, his weapon raised.

T'Kal lay there, dazed and defeated. "This is not over," he said, getting up and limping away. The remaining lizard monsters saw things and followed T'Kal.

The entire area was now filled with chaos and destruction. Pieces of the tree were scattered everywhere, and the once tranquil and peaceful space was now a hazardous warzone.

Cutter watched T'Kal leave, then rushed to Keijo's side and helped her to her feet. "Are you okay?" he asked, a look of concern on his face.

"I'll be fine," Keijo replied, brushing off the dirt from her clothes and limping. "But we need to help the others."

As the Elvians looked around at the destruction wrought by the lizard monsters, there was a sense of sadness and despair in the air. But Alberad was determined not to let the attackers win.

"Everyone, listen to me!" Alberad called out, his voice ringing through the chaos. "We need to start repairing our home and helping the injured. We cannot let them defeat us."

Cutter, who had just checked on Keijo, joined Alberad's side. "I'll gather some wood to start rebuilding the damaged buildings," he said.

"I'll help you," Albwin and Alvin said in unison, grabbing their axes and following Cutter.

Bari approached the Tree of Life and knelt beside it, examining the damage. "We need to protect this tree," she said. "I'm sorry this happened to you."

Alberad concurred in agreement. "We'll set up a perimeter around it to keep it safe. And we'll start caring for the wounded Elvians."

The Elvians sprang into action, working together to rebuild their home and help the injured. There were murmured conversations between them as they worked, discussing how they could prevent this from happening again in the future.

"We need to be more vigilant," one Elvian said. "We can't let our guard down again."

"And we need to train our younger generation to fight and defend themselves," another added.

As the Elvians worked, there was a sense of hope and determination in the air. They may have been beaten down, but they were not defeated. They were determined to rise again and rebuild a stronger, more secure Earnoche.

Chapter 32

Not All Sunshine and Rainbows

As Maldreg, Reibeala, Sadeck, and Gobulir began their journey back through the deep dark vastness of the ocean, they were all on high alert, knowing that they needed to be careful of any potential dangers that might be lurking in the water.

"We need to be on the lookout for whatever attacked Gobulir last time," Maldreg said, his voice tense with worry.

"Yeah, I don't want to have to go through that again," Gobulir replied, his hand unconsciously going to where he was hit.

"We should stick close together," Reibeala suggested. "If something does attack, we'll have a better chance of fighting it off if we're all together."

"Agreed," Maldreg bowed his head, and the four of them huddled close as they continued through the ocean.

They kept a watchful eye out for any signs of danger, but for the most part, their journey was uneventful. However, as they got further from Postis waters, they started to feel a growing sense of unease.

"Do you feel that?" Sadeck asked, looking around nervously. "It feels like we're being watched again."

"I feel it too," Gobulir replied, his eyes darting around as he tried to spot any potential threats.

"We need to stay alert," Maldreg said firmly. "We don't know what might be out here."

They continued on, their nerves on edge, but thankfully, they managed to make it back to the sandy shore without any incidents. As they emerged from the water and onto the shore, they all breathed a sigh of relief.

"We made it," Reibeala said, her voice shaking slightly.

Their relief was short-lived. As they walked on the sandy beach, Maldreg reminded his companions of their next challenge. "We have to make our way back through the harsh desert," he said, reminding them of the dangers that lay ahead.

Sadeck looked around at the barren land stretching out before them. The sun beat down mercilessly, and he could already feel the heat bearing down on him. "This will be a long and difficult journey, take of your suits and put on the heat proof clothing…..quickly" he said.

Maldreg approving, his face grim. "We must be prepared for anything," he added, "and be on the lookout for any sign of danger."

As they started their journey back, they tried to conserve their energy by walking at a steady pace. The sand shifted under their feet, making their steps unstable. The only sounds were the crunching of sand and the occasional muttered curse as someone stumbled.

Gobulir was fascinated by the jewel they had retrieved from the Aquanauts, but his thoughts soon turned to getting home. "Reibeala, how long do you think it'll take to get home?" he asked fearfully.

Reibeala patted his arm comfortingly. "Don't worry, Gobulir. We'll get there soon enough," she said.

The group trudged on through the hot, unforgiving desert, their thoughts focused on making it back to their mountain. The journey was long and arduous, but they finally reached the safety of Cravmod. Exhausted but relieved, they hugged each other and thanked their lucky stars for making it back alive.

As Maldreg, Reibeala, Sadeck, and Gobulir approached their home, they were already imagining the warm welcome that awaited them. They had been on a long and arduous journey, and it was finally coming to an end. The four of them were exhausted, but also excited to share their tales of adventure and success despite some upset.

The climb up the mountain was treacherous, but the four of them were determined to make it back to their home in one piece. Reibeala was the first to reach the top, her strong legs and unwavering determination propelling her forward. Maldreg was next, his powerful arms helping him scale the rocky terrain with ease. Sadeck and Gobulir brought up the rear, their shorter legs struggling to keep up with their more nimble companions.

Once they finally reached the top, they made their way to the great hall. As they entered they were greeted by Brarmuk and Norakor. The two were overjoyed to see their friends had returned safe and sound. Brarmuk greeted them with a warm embrace and a hearty laugh, while Norakor smiled widely and clapped his hands in excitement.

"Welcome back, my friends!" Brarmuk exclaimed. "You have done our people proud with your journey. Come sit down and tell us, what have you seen?"

Maldreg was the first to speak, his deep voice filling the hall. "We have seen wonders beyond our wildest dreams," he said, his eyes shining with excitement. "We found an ocean and it was full of life and beauty, and we even encountered a different race of people called the Aquanauts. They were kind and gracious, and they gave us a gift, a precious gem to bring back."

Reibeala took her turn, her voice filled with wonder. "There were many jewels! They were so breathtakingly beautiful, I've never seen anything like it. The colours were so bright and the way they sparkled in the light was just magical."

Sadeck and Gobulir chimed in, sharing their own experiences from the journey. The two of them were still in awe of the water world they had encountered, and they could not stop talking about the different creatures they had seen and the amazing sights they had witnessed.

Brarmuk and Norakor listened intently to their friends' tales, nodding and smiling in agreement. They were proud of their people for venturing out into the unknown, and for bringing back such a valuable treasure to their home.

"You have done our people proud," Brarmuk said, beaming with pride. "The gem you have brought back may help us."

With that, the four adventurers were welcomed back into their home with open arms, their journey and their bravery celebrated by all. They had made history, and they would always be remembered as the first to venture into the unknown and return with tales of wonder and adventure.

Maldreg had something he needed to share with Brarmuk and Norakor, something that could not wait.

He pulled the two elders aside, "We encountered something dangerous in the water. Gobulir was attacked by a creature, but it disappeared before we could react. Not only the attack but we saw another race of people…... This has me worried, there may be more dangers in the ocean that we do not yet know about."

Norakor whispered to himself, "The tales of the Kraken are whispered among our people, but many believe it to be just a myth."

Brarmuk nodded, "We need to be vigilant on any future expeditions. Our people's safety is of utmost importance."

Maldreg continued, "I think we should keep a watchful eye on the waters. And if anything else happens, we need to be prepared to take action."

Brarmuk and Norakor agreed, "We will make sure our people are informed and prepared. Thank you for bringing this to our attention, Maldreg."

The three of them returned to the main hall, where the mood was still celebratory. But the news of what had happened in the ocean cast a shadow over the festivities, and a sense of unease settled in. The Mountaineers had always known the myth of Kraken, but now they had to face the possibility that it could actually be true.

Reibeala was sitting quietly in the main hall of the mountain, surrounded by her friends and fellow Mountaineers. Despite the joy of their return, she couldn't shake the feeling of unease in the pit of her stomach. She stood up and walked over to Brarmuk.

"Brarmuk," she said, her voice a bit shaky. "What happened to Dugruck? Did he make it back with the others?"

Brarmuk looked at Reibeala with sadness in his eyes. "I'm sorry, Reibeala," he said. "Dugruck did not make it back. The two others returned safely, but Dugruck lost his life on the journey back home."

Reibeala's heart sank. Dugruck was one of her closest friends, and she couldn't bear the thought of losing him. "Why!?" she asked, tears starting to form in her eyes.

Reibeala bit her lip, trying to hold back her tears. She sat back down, lost in thought. She couldn't help but think about the dangers that they faced on their journey, and how they were always one step away from disaster.

She knew that they were brave and strong, but the dangers they faced were becoming more and more real to her. She couldn't help but wonder what other dangers lay ahead, and if they would be able to face them.

As Gobulir made his way back to his friends, he was greeted like royalty. The very small group of only friends he had clapped for him, welcoming him back to their midst.

Gobulir beamed with pride as he told his friends about his journey. However, his story was a heavily exaggerated version of what had actually happened. He told them about the gems he had seen, and how they could use them to upgrade their weaponry.

"My friends, you won't believe what I saw on my journey," Gobulir said, his eyes shining with excitement. "Gems, precious gems. They're just waiting for us to take them. And imagine what we could do with them, upgrade our weapons and make us stronger than ever before!"

His friends listened intently, their eyes wide with wonder.

"But how do we get them?" one of his friends asked.

"We'll have to go and get them," Gobulir replied with a mischievous grin. "We'll go as a small group and go steal those gems. We can do this, I know we can."

"But what if we're caught?" another friend asked, sounding worried.

"Don't worry, I've done this before, we'll be careful. We'll plan everything out and make sure we're not caught," Gobulir said, trying to reassure his friends.

"Okay, let's do it," one of his friends said, sounding determined. "We can't let those gems go to waste."

Gobulir's friends responded with acknowledgement, and soon the group was in the middle of planning their mission to steal the gems. Gobulir was at the centre of it all, relishing in the attention and excitement. It was clear that his journey had not only brought him back to his friends, but it had also brought a new sense of purpose to his life.

Brarmuk approached Sadeck, his trusted engineer, and called him over. Sadeck walked over to him, his eyes fixed on the large gem that Brarmuk was holding in his hand.

"Sadeck," Brarmuk began, "I need your help. I have heard rumours of the dangerous sea creature, known as the Kraken, as you know. It is said to have immense strength and is capable of destroying anything in its path according to myth. We must be prepared for anything, and I need your help to make better armour for our people."

Sadeck took a deep breath and looked at the gem. He knew what Brarmuk was asking of him, and he was nervous about it. He had never worked with gems like this before, and he didn't know if he would be able to make anything useful with it.

"Brarmuk," Sadeck began, "I will do my best, but I have never worked with gems like this before. I will need time to research and study the properties of this gem to see if it is suitable for use in armour or anything else."

Brarmuk responded, "Take the time you need, Sadeck. Our people's safety is of the utmost importance. We cannot risk another attack like what happened to Gobulir."

Sadeck took the diamond from Brarmuk and began to study it. He spent hours examining it, noting its properties and weighing its strengths and weaknesses. He knew that if he was going to make anything useful from it, he would have to work hard and put in a lot of effort.

Sadeck worked tirelessly, his mind focused on creating the perfect armour for the Mountaineers. He knew that this was a big responsibility, and he didn't want to let Brarmuk or the Mountaineers down.

And so, Sadeck began work on it, determined to make the best possible protection for the Mountaineers against whatever dangers they might face in the future.

Chapter 33

Toru's Disobedience

Toru walked along the coral reef, his head hanging low. He couldn't believe that Triton had sent him back home during their mission. He had worked so hard to prove himself, but in the end, it was all for nothing. As he walked, he talked to himself, venting his frustration.

"Why did Triton send me back? I thought I had done well on our mission. I was sure I had proven myself. And now I'm back here, stuck on the shore of Postis" Toru muttered to himself.

As he walked, he came across Nixie and Ari. They were busy with their daily chores, collecting shells and seaweed for their homes. Toru tried to hide his disappointment, but Nixie and Ari could see that something was wrong.

"What's wrong, Toru? Why are you so down?" Nixie asked, her tone filled with concern.

"Triton sent us back. Doesn't that bother you?" Toru replied, his voice heavy with sadness.

Ari put a hand on his shoulder, trying to offer some comfort. "It's okay, Toru. We'll get there."

But Toru wasn't so sure. He couldn't shake the feeling that he was never going to be good enough, that he was never going to be allowed to explore the open ocean.

As Nixie and Ari went back to their chores, Toru continued to walk along the coral reef, lost in his thoughts. He didn't know what the future held for him.

Toru swam out into the open ocean, feeling angry and frustrated. He hated being stuck at home, and he hated Triton for sending him back.

"This is pointless," he muttered to himself. "I hate it here. I hate being told what to do all the time."

He continued to swim, his anger and frustration growing with each passing stroke of ocean water. He didn't understand why Triton always seemed to treat him differently than the other Aquanauts.

"I'm just as good as they are," he thought. "Why can't I explore and have adventures like the rest of them?"

As he swam further out, he began to feel a sense of freedom. The open ocean was vast and endless, and for the first time, he felt like he was truly in control.

"I don't need Triton or anyone else to tell me what to do," he said to himself. "I can do whatever I want."

And with that, he continued to swim, determined to explore and discover new things in the ocean. He may have been sent home, but he wasn't going to let that stop him from having adventures of his own.

Toru swam further and further away from the reef, the rush of the ocean giving him a sense of freedom and escape from his mundane life. But as he continued on, he started to realize the danger of his situation. The sky was darkening, and he could feel the wind picking up speed.

"I shouldn't have come out here. I should have stayed back on the reef," Toru thought to himself as he started to feel uneasy about the situation.

Suddenly, the waves started to become more intense. The water was getting rougher and the current was getting stronger. The wind was howling, and the rain was starting to pour down. Toru struggled to stay afloat as he was being pushed and pulled by the powerful waves.

He tried to swim back towards the reef, but the current was too strong. The waves were getting higher, and he was being thrown around like a leaf in the wind. Toru's arms and legs started to tire, and he was quickly becoming exhausted.

He disappeared under the water, the waves and current too strong for him to fight against. He could feel himself being pulled deeper and deeper into the ocean. The sound of the storm faded away as he was consumed by the dark and murky depths of the ocean.

"I should have listened to Triton. I should have stayed safe. I shouldn't have let my anger control me," Toru thought as he felt himself being pulled further and further away from the surface.

Nixie and Ari were walking along the shore when they noticed the storm quickly approaching. They looked out to the coral where they saw him last, but there was no sign of Toru.

"Do you think he went home?" Nixie asked Ari, who shrugged. "Probably," Ari said.

"He was sulking earlier and probably just went home."

But as the storm worsened, Nixie couldn't shake the feeling that something was wrong. She had a sense of foreboding that she couldn't ignore.

"I hope he's okay," Nixie said, looking out to the ocean. "These currents can be really strong during a storm."

"Don't worry, Nixie," Ari replied, trying to reassure her.

Chapter 34

Bari's Vision

Bari woke up in the jet black darkness of the night, quickly sitting up and gasping for air. She had a vivid vision of Kraken again. Kraken was attacking a group of flying Wyvinites she had never seen before. In the vision, she saw a clear path to the Wyvinites.

She sat up in her bed, her heart racing with fear and excitement. She couldn't shake the image of Kraken from her mind and the urgency she felt to find the Wyvinites and to warn them.

Bari got out of bed and made her way to the tree houses, where most of her people were still asleep. She found Alberad and Cutter and woke them up, telling them about her vision.

"Kraken is going to attack, I have seen it in my vision. Kraken is real!" Bari said, her voice filled with worry. "And I saw a way to a place where flying Wyvinites are. We have to go and find them. They are the Key"

Alberad rubbed his eyes, trying to wake up fully. "Wyvinites? What do they have to do with this?"

"I don't know," Bari replied. "But in my vision, they were the key to stopping Kraken. We have to go and find them."

Alberad showed understanding but with slight confusion. "We'll gather the others and set out at first light. We will not lose any more of our home"

Bari smiled, grateful for their support. She felt the weight of responsibility on her shoulders, but she was determined to find the Wyvinites and stop Kraken before it was too late.

Chapter 35

The Search for the Wyvinites

As the sun rose in the pink and orange morning sky, Alberad gathered Cutter, Bari, Albwin, Alvin, and Keijo in the centre of Earnoche. He looked at each of them, his eyes filled with determination and curiosity.

"Friends, Bari has had a vision…. We have to leave on a search for the people she saw… The Wyvinites," Alberad began. "It will be dangerous, but we have to do this. We have to find out what's going on in the world."

Although confused at the hearing of Wyvinites they all knew they did not want another disaster so they all showed conformity in their agreement.

"Bari," Alberad said, turning to her. "You will be leading the way. You are our map."

Bari looked at him, her eyes wide. "Me?" she said, her voice filled with fear.

"Yes, you," Alberad said firmly. "You have seen the way in your vision, that will guide us to the Wyvinites. We need you."

Bari took a deep breath and bowed her head. "Okay," she said. "I'll do my best."

"Good," Alberad said. "We'll leave in two hours. Get ready."

As they all went off to prepare for the journey, Alberad couldn't help but think of the danger that lay ahead. But he knew they had to find out what was happening in the world, and the Wyvinites were their only hope.

He just hoped they would be ready for what they might find.

The group of Alberad, Cutter, Bari, Albwin, Alvin, and Keijo set off and after a while trekking through the forest they approached the edge of Earnoche, they could hear the sound of a rushing river ahead. Alberad spoke up, "No one has ever passed this river before. It is said to be impassable, but Bari will be leading the way as she is our map."

Bari stepped forward, her eyes fixed on the river ahead. "I saw a tree in my vision," she said. "It's over there, near the river's edge."

Cutter looked sceptically at the raging waters, "How are we supposed to cross that?

"We'll find a way," said Alberad confidently. "We have Bari leading us, and she has seen the way through."

"But what if there is no way across?" asked Albwin.

"We'll make a way," replied Keijo. "We won't let a river stop us from reaching our goal."

The group moved towards the tree, their eyes on the raging waters. Bari stepped forward and began to lead them towards the tree, her feet finding sure footing on the floor covered in uneven roots. They approached the magnificently massive tree that was bent over the rushing river and Bari reached out to touch it.

"This is it," she said. "This is what I saw in my vision."

"How are we supposed to get across the river now?" asked Alvin, his voice filled with fear.

Bari looked out over the rushing waters and closed her eyes. She had seen in her vision. The rest of the group followed closely behind, their eyes fixed on the towering structure in front of them. "We climb" She said.

Alberad spoke up, his voice filled with concern.

"This tree looks wobbly, are you sure it's safe to climb?"

Bari nodded, her confidence unwavering. "In my vision, I saw this tree as our way to cross the river. We have to trust it."

Albwin, who was usually the first to speak, was uncharacteristically quiet. Cutter, who was known for his bravery, looked a little uneasy. Keijo and Alvin, however, were determined to see this through.

As they started to climb, the tree swayed with their weight. The wind picked up, causing the branches to sway even more. Bari held on tight, her grip steady. Suddenly, one of the group members, Cutter, lost his balance and was about to fall into the rushing water below.

"Hold on!" Keijo cried, reaching out to grab Cutter's hand.

Cutter grabbed Keijo's hand and managed to steady himself. "Thanks," he panted, his heart racing.

"We have to be careful," Alberad warned, his voice stern. "One misstep and we could all be lost."

Alberad led the way across the tree, his eyes fixed on the far shore. The group followed, their steps steady and sure as they crossed, their progress slower now as they made their way over the river. When they finally made it to the other side, they all let out a collective sigh of relief.

"We made it," Alvin said, his voice filled with wonder.

Bari smiled, her eyes shining with determination. "Let's keep going. The Wyvinites are waiting for us."

"We're one step closer," said Alberad, a smile spreading across his face. "Let's keep moving forward."

With that, they set off once again, their journey to find the Wyvinites continuing. The wind may have been strong, but their resolve was even stronger.

As they continued on their journey, the terrain around them gradually began to change. The lush green trees with their roots firmly planted on the ground began to thin out, replaced by rockier, more barren terrain. The group was amazed at the sight of the towering volcano that loomed in the distance.

"Wow," breathed Bari, leading the group forward. "This is Wyvinite, the volcano that sits at the centre of the Wyvinites territory."

"It's beautiful," said Keijo, shielding her eyes for a moment from the intense brightness radiating from the lava that flowed down the side of the volcano.

"But also dangerous," added Albwin, eyeing the volcano warily. "We have to be careful if we're going to get close to it."

"Don't worry," said Bari, with a confident smile. "I saw the way in my vision. I'll lead us there."

"I hope so," said Alvin, a hint of unease in his voice. "I don't want to get caught in the middle of an eruption."

"Me neither," said Cutter, his eyes fixed on the volcano. "Let's just get this over with."

The group continued on, their conversations halting as they were in awe of the towering volcano in front of them. They were nervous but excited to finally meet the Wyvinites, hoping they could help them defeat Kraken and save their people.

As Bari led the group through the open gates of Wyvinite, their excitement turned to disappointment as they found the bustling city she had seen in her vision was now empty and silent.

Alberad was the first to speak with disappointment. "I don't see anyone here. Perhaps your vision was wrong, Bari."

Bari shook her head, determined. "No, I'm sure they lived here. I saw it so clearly."

Cutter spoke up, his voice filled with concern. "What could have happened to them? They must have gone somewhere."

Alvin added, "We should split up and search the city. Maybe they went to the outskirts."

Albwin agreed, "Yes, we can cover more ground that way."

Keijo agreed, "We should be careful though, the terrain is rocky and it could be dangerous."

Bari took a deep breath, "I'll lead the way." She started to move forward, her eyes scanning the empty chambers for any signs of life.

Alberad placed a hand on her shoulder, "Are you sure, Bari? It's a big responsibility."

Bari smiled nervously, "I have the vision to guide us. I know what to do."

And so, the group prepared to split up and set out to search the empty city of Wyvinite, hoping to find some answers to the mysterious disappearance of the Wyvinites.

Chapter 36

Hide and Seek

Nozos stood at the top of the volcano, scanning the distant horizon. Suddenly, he spotted something that made his blood run cold: a group of unfamiliar creatures were making their way towards Wyvinite.

He quickly made his way back down the volcano to find Zerig and Qyvrag.

"Zerig, Qyvrag," Nozos said, his voice urgent, "I've seen something out there. A group of creatures I've never seen before are headed this way. We need to get everyone to hide. We will not be attacked again. We will surprise them"

Zerig and Qyvrag both frowned, looking out at the horizon to see what Nozos had seen. They could see nothing yet, but they trusted Nozos's judgement.

"Alright," Zerig said, "We'll gather everyone and bring them to the chamber. It's the only place where we can hide and not be seen."

Nozos made his way to the central chamber, where the rest of the Wyvinites were gathered. Zerig explained the situation to everyone ensuring they followed instructions and were hiding behind the heavy stone doors.

"Everyone, stay quiet and stay hidden," Zerig whispered, "We don't know what these creatures are and we don't want to take any chances."

As the group of creatures approached, the Wyvinites held their breath, listening as the sounds of footsteps and voices grew louder. But after a few moments, the sounds faded a little, and it was clear that the creatures had not found them.

Nozos and Qyvrag were standing at the entrance of the chamber, listening to Alvin the Elvian as he spoke about splitting up. Nozos leaned over to Qyvrag and whispered a plan to attack once they had split up.

"Qyvrag, once they have split up, we'll have the advantage. We'll attack them one by one and quickly take control," Nozos whispered.

But Qyvrag was growing impatient. He was eager to face the unknown group and defend their home. Without a word, he burst out of the chamber and towards the incoming group. Nozos and the rest of the Wyvinites quickly followed.

As they approached the unknown group, Qyvrag let out a battle cry. The group turned to face them and Nozos could see they were not friendly. He spread his wings, ready for the fight.

"Stay together! We'll fight as a team," Nozos yelled.

As Qyvrag attacked Alvin the Elvian, the rest of the Wyvinites followed suit, ready for a fight. But Bari, who was brave and determined, stepped forward with her hands raised in the air.

"STOP!" she yelled, trying to calm the situation. "We're here to help, not to harm."

The Wyvinites, caught off guard by Bari's sudden intervention and boldness, hesitated for a moment. They looked at each other, unsure of what to do next.

Alberad, who had been furthest away, stepped forward to stand by Bari's side. "Yes, we come in peace," he said, trying to calm the situation. "We have come to help against the threat of Kraken."

Nozos, who had been listening from a distance, spoke up. "What threat of Kraken, what is this Kraken?" he asked, looking at the group sceptically.

"You are in grave danger".

Bari stepped forward and explained everything they had learned about the rumours of Kraken and their journey to find the Wyvinites. She told them about the visions she had had and how she was sure they would be able to help.

The Wyvinites listened intently, their expressions changing from scepticism to interest as Bari spoke.

"Come forth," said Nozos, speaking up after a moment of consideration. "Come, let us discuss this further in our council chamber."

As Cutter went to pick Alvin up, the injured Elvian, he noticed a field beaming with crops behind the council chamber.

They all walked into the chamber and sat down. He was amazed by the abundance of life and felt a sense of hope.

"We could use the Wyvinites strength and the Elvians knowledge," Alberad said, bringing everyone's attention back to the matter at hand. "Together, we could defeat anything in our way."

Bari stepped forward, her eyes shining with determination. "My vision showed us all working together, fighting side by side against the Kraken. It's why we're here."

"But first," Keijo interjected, "we need to understand each other's strengths and weaknesses. Only then can we defeat Kraken."

Alberad responded in agreement. "Bari, please explain your vision to us all. We need to know exactly what we're up against."

Bari took a deep breath and started explaining her vision. She told them of Kraken attacking and destroying everything in its path, and of the Elvians and Wyvinites working together to defeat it. She told them of the importance of their unity and how they could not defeat Kraken alone.

The council chamber was silent as they all absorbed the information. Then, one by one, they started nodding in agreement.

"We have to work together," Albwin said, determination in his voice. "We can't let the Kraken destroy our home."

"Agreed," Alvin said, his voice weak but determined. "I may be injured, but I will do all I can to help."

With their minds set on the task ahead, the Elvians and Wyvinites began to strategize and plan. They discussed their strengths, weaknesses and what each group could bring to the table. They worked on creating a solid plan to defeat the Kraken and protect their home.

The atmosphere was tense. The Elvians, Alberad, Bari, Alvin, Albwin, Cutter, and Keijo, were united in their desire to defeat Kraken, but Nozos, the leader of the Wyvinites, had other ideas.

"If we are to agree to take down Kraken, we need some sort of deal," Nozos said firmly. "We have strength and power, but we cannot simply give it away for free."

The Elvians exchanged worried glances, unsure of what Nozos was asking for.

"What do you have to offer?" Nozos continued, his eyes fixed on Alberad.

Alberad took a deep breath, considering the question carefully. "We have knowledge, experience, and wood," he said. "But most of all, we have the desire to protect the world and all its inhabitants."

Nozos nodded thoughtfully, but it was clear that he was not satisfied. "Wood," he said finally. "We will need wood for fortifications, and we will need it in large quantities, every month!"

Cutter looked disappointed at the request. He had worked hard to gather and cultivate the wood, and the thought of giving it away was difficult for him.

Alberad hesitated, knowing that Nozos was asking for too much. "I'm sorry, Nozos," he said finally. "We cannot give away that much wood. It is a valuable resource, and we need it for our own use as well."

Nozos sighed, clearly disappointed. "Very well," he said. "It seems we cannot come to a deal after all. We will go our separate ways, and we will take care of Kraken on our own."

The Elvians stood up, feeling defeated. They had come so close to securing the help of the Wyvinites, but in the end, it seemed that they would have to face Kraken alone.

Bivis, probably the smartest of all the Wyvinites, sat quietly in the back of the council chamber, listening to the negotiations between the Elvians and the Wyvinites. As he heard the talk of the impending danger he feared that their fields of crops might be destroyed, he grew increasingly worried.

He thought to himself, "What if our land is destroyed and our fields are ruined? We need to protect our food and resources, just in case. We can't rely on the Elvians for help now."

With determination in his heart, Bivis made a decision. He would build a pantry deep within the volcano, where it would be safe and protected from any danger.

Bivis set to work immediately, gathering supplies and tools from around the Wyvinite. He would work tirelessly, determined to complete the pantry as soon as possible. He would dig deep into the volcano, using the lava as a source of heat and light, and build a secure storage room to protect their food and resources.

As he worked, Bivis talked to himself, "I know it's risky, but it's worth it to protect our future. We can't afford to lose everything we've worked so hard for. I'll make sure this pantry is strong enough to withstand anything that comes our way."

Despite the danger and the difficulties he faced, Bivis persevered. He was determined to complete the pantry and make sure that his people would be protected in the event of any disaster.

The Elvians journeyed back to Earnoche with heavy hearts, their mission to ally with the Wyvinites had been unsuccessful. Despite their bravery and Bari's valiant efforts to communicate with the Wyvinites, their requests for assistance in defeating Kraken had been met with resistance.

As they travelled, Alberad walked alongside Bari, deep in thought. "We need to come up with a new plan," he said, breaking the silence. "Kraken won't wait for us."

"I agree," Bari replied. "But I don't know what else we can do. The Wyvinites seemed very set in their ways, and their land is so isolated from the rest of the world."

Cutter chimed in, "We could try to find other allies. Maybe there are others out there who would be willing to help us."

"That's a good idea," Albwin said. "But where would we even start looking?"

Alvin added, "And time is not on our side. We need to act quickly if we want to have any chance of defeating Kraken."

Keijo responded with understanding, "We'll need to put our heads together and come up with a new strategy."

As they continued their journey, the conversations continued. They discussed various possibilities, but no clear solution presented itself. Despite the challenges ahead, the Elvians remained determined to find a way to defeat Kraken and protect their home.

As they approached the edge of Earnoche, the lush green trees with roots on the floor welcomed them back. Despite the disappointment of their mission, the beauty of their home provided comfort. The Elvians knew they had a long road ahead, but they were up for the challenge. They were ready to work together and find a way to defeat the mighty Kraken and protect their home.

The Elvians made their way back to the tree that Bari had led them to in order to cross the rushing river. As they started to make their way back across the wobbly tree, Keijo was the last in line. She was nervous as she stepped on the first branch, it swayed beneath her feet causing her to wobble. She reached for the next branch but it was just out of reach, she started to panic and her grip on the branch began to loosen. The branch slipped from her grasp.

Just then, Cutter, who was just ahead of her, turned around just in time. He quickly made his way back towards her, reaching out a hand to catch her.

"Don't worry Keijo, I've got you," Cutter said, his voice firm and steady as he caught her at the last second.

Keijo grabbed his hand, relief washing over her as Cutter pulled her up to a stable branch.

"Thanks, Cutter," Keijo said, her voice shaking tremendously. "I don't know what would have happened if you weren't here."

"No problem," Cutter replied with a grin. "I'll always be here to catch you."

The group continued to make their way across the tree, the wind picked up causing the tree to sway even more, but they all held on tight, finally reaching the other side of the river safely.

Alberad breathed a sigh of relief as they all made it across the river and onto solid ground. "That was a close call," he said, looking back at the tree. "But we made it. We're home."

Chapter 37

The Search for Toru

The storm had finally settled down in Postis and Nixie and Ari took advantage of the break in the weather to look for Toru. They searched the beach, they swam the local waters and even searched within the coral reefs for him. There was no sight or any sign of him after searching for hours. Nixie and Ari started to get worried. They were sad at the thought of never seeing Toru again so decided to go and tell Triton.

Triton listened intently to Nixie and Ari's concerns, then gathered Roka and Zale to go and search for Toru. The five of them scoured the beach and the nearby coral but still couldn't find any sign of Toru.

"He could have gone anywhere," Nixie said, her voice filled with worry. "We need to expand our search."

"I agree," Triton said. "Let's split up and cover more ground. We'll meet back here in an hour."

Roka went to the north, Zale went to the south, Nixie and Ari went to the east, and Triton went to the west. They searched for hours, calling Toru's name and looking for any signs of him. But no matter how hard they tried, they couldn't find him.

As the sun began to set, the four of them reconvened back at the beach, empty-handed and filled with frustration.

"What if something happened to him?" Nixie asked, tears starting to form in her eyes.

"Don't worry, Nixie," Triton said, placing a comforting hand on her shoulder. "We'll find him. We just need to keep searching."

"But what if we don't?" Roka asked, her voice filled with concern. "What if he's hurt or lost or... something worse?"

"Don't think like that," Zale said, trying to be positive. "Toru is a strong swimmer. He can take care of himself."

But despite their reassurances, the five of them couldn't shake the feeling of worry that hung over them like a cloud.

They continued their search for Toru, determined to bring him back home safe and sound.

"We need to keep searching," Nixie said, "We can't give up until we find him."

Roka was at the front of the search, using her navigational skills to push them forward in their hunt for Toru.

As they swam deeper and further out, they stumbled across a cave system they had never seen before. It looked mysterious, dark and a little creepy. The entrance was covered in markings that could only have been made by a massive creature, and they wondered what sort of creature could have made them.

They were cared of what could be within the cave system but determined to find Toru, so the group swam inside the caves. They explored the twisting, narrow tunnels trying their hardest to remember the route they had taken so they wouldn't become lost inside. After several twist and turns through the narrow cave system they stumbled upon what looked like an air pocket. They approached with caution readying themselves for the worst. They slowly emerged from the water. Roka could not believe her eyes. Inside, they found Toru huddled up in a ball.

"Toru!" Roka cried, relief flooding over her. "We found you!"

Toru looked up at them, a weak smile on his face. "I'm so glad you found me," he said, his voice shaking and tears rolling down his face. The group embraced each other for a moment until Triton interrupted the moment. "We need to make our way back, it is dark and we don't know if we are alone in these caves."

As they swam back to Postis, they talked about the mysterious caves they had found. They were amazed by the intricate markings and couldn't help but wonder what kind of creature could have created them.

"Who or what lives in those caves," Triton said.

The group shuddered at the thought in silence. They then returned to Postis, grateful to have found Toru safe and sound. They knew that there were still many mysteries to uncover in the ocean, but for now, they were just happy to be reunited with their friend.

Chapter 38

Gobulir's Adventure

Gobulir was in deep thought as he sat with his friends, Ash and Kalt, discussing their next move. They needed to acquire the rare gems from the Aquanauts and Gobulir had a plan.

"We need to sneak into Sadeck's workshop and take the heat proof clothing and underwater gear," Gobulir declared. "We'll use that to venture through the desert and in the ocean."

"That's risky," Ash warned. "Sadeck will notice if his gear is missing."

"Not if we're careful," Gobulir replied confidently. "We'll leave no traces."

Kalt beamed in agreement, eager for the adventure. "I'm in, let's do it."

Later that night, Gobulir sneaked into Sadeck's workshop and gathered the gear as planned. He quickly returned to the small group that were waiting for him in anticipation.

"We're all set," Gobulir whispered as he handed out the gear. "Let's go."

Gobulir, Ash, and Kalt made their way through the scorching hot desert, their eyes fixed on the distant horizon where they could just make out the glimmer of the ocean. Their journey had been a long one, filled with danger and uncertainty, but they were determined to reach their goal and claim the gems from the Aquanauts.

As they trudged through the sand, the three friends chatted about their mission and the obstacles they might face along the way. Gobulir, the boldest of the three, was confident that they would succeed. "We've come this far," he said, "We can make it the rest of the way."

Ash, ever the sceptic, wasn't so sure. "What if the Aquanauts have already claimed the gems?" she asked.

Kalt, the quietest of the group, simply shrugged and replied, "Then we'll find another way to get what we want."

The three friends continued on, the hot sun beating down on their backs. They took turns carrying the heavy gear and supplies, pausing every so often to take a drink from their water skins.

As they approached the ocean, the scenery changed from barren desert to beautiful blue waters. The air grew cooler and the sound of crashing waves filled their ears. They quickened their pace, eager to finally reach the ocean and begin their search for the gems.

Upon reaching the shore, they stood in awe at the vast expanse of water stretching out before them. Gobulir turned to his friends and said, "We are half way there! Half way to getting those gems."

Ash and Kalt smiled in agreement, and the three friends put on their underwater equipment on and stepped into the water, ready to begin their search. They were filled with excitement and determination, knowing that their journey was far from over, but that the reward would be worth it in the end.

Gobulir stood at the edge of the water, the waves lapping at his feet. He gazed out at the endless expanse of blue, memories of his last journey here flooding his mind. He had been attacked from behind when he was deep at the bottom of the ocean and he didn't want the same fate to befall his friends.

He turned to Ash and Kalt, who were eagerly waiting to dive in. Gobulir took a deep breath and spoke in a serious tone, "Be careful, this is where I was attacked last time. Be vigilant and stay close."

Ash looked at Gobulir with concern, "What happened again?"

"I encountered a group of sea monsters that were unlike anything in existence. I barely escaped with my life." Gobulir replied exaggerating, his voice still haunted by the experience.

Kalt looked sceptical, "Are you sure it's safe for us to go in?"

Gobulir nodded firmly, "We have to. We need those gems. We'll be fine as long as we stick together and watch each other's backs."

Ash and Kalt exchanged a look, and then signalled their agreement. They knew the importance of their mission and they were willing to face any danger to complete it.

"Let's do this," Ash said, determination in his voice.

The three friends splashed into the water, their gear making them feel heavy. Gobulir led the way, his eyes scanning the surrounding area for any signs of danger. They swam deeper into the ocean, the water growing colder and darker.

"Stay alert," Gobulir warned, his voice echoing through the water. "We don't know what's down here."

Ash and Kalt scanning too, their hearts beating fast with anticipation and fear. They continued to swim, each of them keeping a watchful eye out for any threats. They didn't know what dangers lay ahead, but they were determined to see their mission through to the end.

Gobulir led Ash and Kalt through the dark waters of the ocean. He knew this area well, as it was where he had encountered a dangerous creature during his previous trip. He cautiously made his way towards the large coral formations that rose up from the ocean floor.

"That's it! That's where I saw the gems," Gobulir exclaimed, pointing to a group of rocks.

Ash and Kalt followed his gaze and saw various gems glistening in the sunlight that filtered down through the water. They marvelled at the beauty of the gems and the way they seemed to glow in the ocean's light.

"Gobulir, I've never seen anything like this before," Kalt said in amazement.

"Me neither," Ash added.

Gobulir smiled, happy to have shared this wondrous sight with his friends. "We need to be careful though. This area is known to be inhabited by the Aquanauts that guard the gems," he warned.

"What do we do?" asked Kalt.

"We'll have to be quick and quiet," Gobulir replied. "We can collect as many gems as we can carry, but we have to be mindful of our surroundings at all times."

The three friends made their way towards the rocks, their eyes fixed on the glistening gems. They picked their way through the coral, disturbing all of the fish that lived among the rocks.

"Look! Over there!" Ash pointed to a large cave that was hidden behind the rocks.

"That's where the gems must be coming from," Gobulir said, excitement in his voice.

The three of them approached the cave, their hearts racing with excitement. They peered inside and saw a large chamber filled with glittering gems of all shapes and sizes.

"We did it! We found the gems!" Gobulir shouted, a wide smile spreading across his face.

"We're rich!" Ash exclaimed, grabbing as many gems as he could carry.

"But we have to be careful," Kalt warned. "We don't want to anger the Aquanauts that live here."

The three friends quickly gathered as many gems as they could carry, carefully making their way back to the surface. They emerged from the water, grinning from ear to ear, their bags filled with the valuable gems.

"Let's go back to Cravmod and show everyone our haul," Gobulir said, starting to lead the group back.

Ash and Kalt followed, their hearts filled with excitement at the thought of all the riches that lay ahead of them. They had successfully found the gems, and now, their future was filled with endless possibilities.

They were suddenly interrupted by the Aquanaut Naia.

"What are you doing here?" Naia demanded, swimming over to them.

"We're here for the gems," Gobulir answered, pushing Naia out of the way.

"You can't just take what's not yours!" Naia yelled, trying to grab Gobulir.

As Naia lunged forward trying to grab Gobulir, Gobulir pushed forward and pushed her backwards. Naia fell and hit her head on the solid rock behind her.

"Go, go, go!" Gobulir shouted to Ash and Kalt, and the three of them quickly swam away, leaving Naia behind.

"She's injured, we need to help her," Ash said, looking back at Naia who was struggling to make it back out of the waters.

"We can't risk getting caught," Gobulir replied, his voice firm. "We need to get out of here and get these gems back to Cravmod. We've come too far to turn back now."

Kalt did not disapprove, and the three of them continued to swim away, leaving Naia behind. They were focused on their mission.

As they swam back to the surface, they could hear Naia shouting for help, but they ignored it and continued on their way.

Ash and Kalt, their faces showing their excitement. They had achieved what they set out to do, and they were proud of themselves. But as they looked at each other, they couldn't help but feel a twinge of guilt for leaving Naia behind.

Chapter 39

The Hard Reality

Alberad, the leader of the Elvians, was sitting in Earnoche's main hall deep in thought. The recent events with the Wyvinites and their failed negotiation with Nozos weighed heavily on his mind. He was joined by Bari, Cutter and Alvin. They had gathered to discuss the situation at hand.

"We cannot defend against Kraken on our own," Alberad stated sombrely. "We need the strength of the Wyvinites."

Bari nodded with verification. "I saw it in my vision. We will need their help to defeat anything that comes our way."

Cutter looked down, disappointment etched on his face. "But I thought our offer of wood would be enough. Why did Nozos ask for so much?"

Alvin sighed. "Nozos's people have been through a lot. They need to fortify their land and they see our offer of wood as valuable. I can understand where he's coming from."

Alberad leaned back in his chair. "Unfortunately, if we accept the offer we don't know how long we stand by that offer!"

The group fell into a heavy silence, each lost in their own thoughts. They knew that the road ahead would be a difficult one, but they also knew that they couldn't give up. They needed to find a way to protect their land and their people from the wrath of Kraken.

"We have to accept Nozos's offer," Alberad said finally after a minute of thought and silence. "We cannot defend against Kraken on our own. We need their strength."

Bari, Cutter, and Alvin showed agreement, understanding the gravity of the situation. They all knew that this was their only option, but it wouldn't be an easy one. They would need to find a way to get the wood to Nozos.

"We will do what we must to protect our land and our people," Alberad declared resolutely. "We will find the way."

The group stood, ready to face the challenges ahead and work towards a solution that would ensure the safety of their people. They knew it wouldn't be easy, but they were determined to do what was necessary to protect their home.

Alberad continued his conversation with Bari, Cutter and Alvin, discussing the best way to transport the wood to Wyvinite. "I don't think our arms and backs would be able to handle such a heavy load, all that way!" Alberad said, stroking his beard.

"Agreed," Cutter chimed in. "We'll need to find a way to transport it over the river and through the forest."

Just then, Bari jolted back in her seat, her eyes going wild. She was in a trance, and the others watched as she muttered to herself.

"What's happening to her?" Alvin asked, concerned.

"She's having a vision," Alberad replied, his voice hushed.

A few moments later, Bari's eyes cleared, and she took a deep breath. "I've seen it," she said, her voice shaking. "We need to take a boat to transport the wood to Wyvinite."

"A boat?" Cutter asked, surprised. "But we've never sailed before. How would we know how to do it?"

"I don't know," Bari replied, still a bit shaken. "But that's what I saw in my vision. We must take a boat."

Alberad stood up, his expression serious. "Then we must start preparing. We'll need to find a way to get our hands on a boat and make sure it's seaworthy."

"And we'll need a crew to man it," Alvin added.

"I'll start making inquiries," Cutter said, already heading for the door. "We'll make this work, no matter what."

"Agreed," Alberad said, determination in his voice. "We must succeed in our mission, for the good of our people."

They continued to discuss their plans, the uncertainty of the journey ahead hanging in the air. But they were determined to make it work, for the sake of their land and their people.

Cutter was now on a mission. He was now marching around Earnoche. He had been asking everyone in sight about a boat but no one seemed to have one or even know where to find one. The idea of transporting the wood to Wyvinite by sea was their only option, but they needed a vessel to make it happen.

As he walked through the village, still determined, he approached Elegast, a seasoned woodworker. Cutter asked him "Do you have any ideas on where we could find a boat?"

"I've been working on a small, handcrafted Teak boat," Elegast replied. "It's not much, but it should be seaworthy."

Cutter's eyes lit up. "Can I take a look at it?"

Elegast led Cutter to the outskirts of the village where he had been working on the boat. It was a small but sturdy vessel, perfect for the task at hand. Cutter ran his hand along the smooth, polished wood and admired Elegast's handiwork.

"This is exactly what we need," Cutter said, looking at Elegast with appreciation. "What do you need from us to get it out to the river?"

"Just a few supplies and a few strong hands to help me move it," Elegast replied.

Cutter grinned, grateful for Elegast's help. "I'll gather the supplies and find some volunteers to help us. We'll have this boat ready and on the river in no time."

Elegast smiled, "happy to be of assistance." He said.

Cutter thanked Elegast and set off to gather the necessary supplies and volunteers. With Elegast's boat, they now had a way to transport the wood to Wyvinite. The task ahead of them was still daunting, but with each step forward, they were one step closer to their goal.

Cutter was filled with excitement as he ran as fast as he could to find Alberad, Bari, and Alvin. He knew he had to tell them about the small boat Elegast had made by hand. The news could be the solution to their problem of how to transport the wood to Wyvinite.

"Alberad, Bari, Alvin!" Cutter called out, panting from his run. "I have some good news!"

Alberad turned to Cutter, a look of hope in his eyes. "What good news?"

"Elegast has a small boat!" Cutter exclaimed. "He's been working on it for some time now. It's a handcrafted wooden boat and it's ready for us to use."

Bari's eyes lit up with excitement. "That's amazing news, Cutter! It's exactly what we needed."

Alberad agreed, a determined look in his eyes. "We'll leave right away. We don't have any time to waste."

Cutter smiled, relieved that his discovery had been met with such enthusiasm. "Elegast is waiting for us in his workshop at the edge of Earnoche. We can go see it now."

Alberad turned to Bari and Alvin. "Let's gather Keijo, Albwin and what we need and head down there. The sooner we leave, the better."

Cutter interrupted "The boat is small and we only have a small amount of space to transport the wood, I think it will only hold four of us."

Alberad sighed, knowing that the larger number of them the safer they would be. "Why must there always be obstacles!" He said with frustration. "We must leave now, us four. Let's go."

As they made their way there, Cutter couldn't help but feel a sense of pride. He had found the solution to their problem, and he had done it by listening and searching for answers. When they arrived, Elegast was waiting for them with the small wooden boat.

"It's not the biggest boat," Elegast said as they approached, "but it's sturdy and seaworthy. It should be able to transport the wood to Wyvinite without any issues."

Alberad, looking impressed. "It's perfect, Elegast. Thank you for your hard work."

Elegast smiled, happy to have been able to help. "I'm glad I could be of assistance. Let's get ready to set sail."

Alberad looked at Elegast, with sorrow "You're not coming with us, there is not enough room and we have already been to Wyvinite, I'm not risking you on this journey."

Elegast devastated at this news but trying to play it off, stepped backed waving his hand in the air "no worries Sir I will see you all soon."

Cutter, Alberad, Bari, Alvin and Elegast stood near the edge of the river, looking down at the handcrafted wooden boat that was meant to transport them and the precious load of wood to Wyvinite but getting it into the water was proving to be a difficult task.

"We need to push it together, on the count of three," Cutter said, getting into position.

"One, two, three!"

The five of them put all their strength into pushing the boat, but it barely moved. They tried again, this time with more force, but still to no avail.

"It's not budging," Alberad said, sweat beading on his brow.

"We need to try again," Bari added, determination in her voice.

They tried once more, this time with all their might. The boat inched forward, then suddenly it gave way and began to move easier. The five of them pushed it to the edge of the river, and then, with a final heave, they launched the boat into the water.

"It's in!" Cutter cried, relief in his voice.

"Good job, everyone," Alberad said, clapping his hands.

"We did it," Elegast added, smiling.

"Now, let's get on board," Alvin said, jumping into the boat.

The rest of them climbed in, taking their seats and grabbing the oars. They set off, the boat gliding through the water, the cool spray of the river hitting their faces. They paddled with determination, the boat moving faster and faster as they gained momentum.

"We're on our way," Bari said, a smile on her face.

The four of them continued to paddle, the boat carrying them towards their destination, their spirits lifted by the success of their launch. Whilst Elegast stood at the edge of the river waving goodbye with a look of envy on his face.

Chapter 40

A New Alliance

The boat, crafted by hand by Elegast, glided effortlessly through the water as Cutter, Alberad, Bari and Alvin made their way towards Wyvinite. The sound of the water lapping against the sides of the boat filled the air and the sun shone down upon them, giving them warmth. The journey was peaceful, allowing them to reflect on the events that had led them here.

As they approached the island of Wyvinite, they could see the familiar figure of Nozos waiting for them on the shore. Cutter, Alberad, Bari, and Alvin disembarked from the boat and approached Nozos with the wood they had brought as promised.

"I wondered if you'd be back," Nozos said with a smirk.

"We have wood," Alberad said as he showed Nozos the logs they had brought. "But we need food in return as well as an alliance."

Nozos rubbed his chin in thought, considering Alberad's request. "I suppose we do have a lot of food. And it's always good to have allies. I guess it's a deal."

The group breathed a collective sigh of relief. They had successfully secured an alliance with the Wyvinites and now had a reliable source of food. They would not have to struggle with hunger any longer.

"Let's go and talk about the details of our agreement," Nozos said as he led the group towards the centre of the island.

As they walked, they discussed the terms of their alliance, making sure to cover every detail. They talked about the amount of food that would be traded for the wood and what would happen if one side did not fulfil their end of the agreement.

After the agreement was made the Elvians started to make their way back to the boat. Cutter, Alberad, Bari, and Alvin, were all relieved as they made their way back to the boat after their successful negotiation with Nozos. The deal was struck and the food they so desperately needed was now secured for their village.

After several hours of rowing had passed, Bari spoke up, "Everyone, let's get some rest. We've had a long day and the river is flowing with us now, so I'll stay awake and keep an eye out."

Cutter said in agreement, "That sounds like a good idea, Bari. I'm exhausted."

Alberad also agreed, "Yes, we all are. We should get some rest."

As they settled into the boat, they began to drift off, lulled by the gentle flow of the river. Bari, who stayed awake, watched over them, her hand resting on the tiller of the boat.

Bari rubbed her eyes and tried to focus on the surrounding landscape, but she felt her eyelids drooping despite her efforts to stay awake. She had been so exhausted from the journey and the events of the day that it was hard for her to keep her eyes open.

But no matter how hard she tried, she felt herself drifting off, her mind slipping into a state of slumber. As she drifted, she saw something in the distance that caught her eye. She rubbed her eyes, thinking it was just a trick of the light, but when she opened them again, she saw it again.

A group of funny looking people, dressed in bulky suits, were walking along the shore in the distance. They looked like they were searching for something, their heads swivelling back and forth as they scanned the area.

And then she saw something even stranger. A small group of people who seemed to shimmer in the sun.

Bari tried to shout to the others to alert them, but her voice was caught in her throat. She tried to move, but her body wouldn't respond. It was as if she was frozen in time, her eyes the only thing that still moved.

And then everything turned black. She had fallen asleep, her mind taking her on an adventure in the realm of dreams.

Bari rubbed her eyes and sat up, looking around. She saw that the boat was docked at the riverbank and everyone else was already disembarking. She heard Cutter's voice as he talked to Alberad.

"Well, we made it back in one piece," Cutter said with a sniggering smile. "Thanks to Bari's watchful eye."

Alberad responded. "Yes, it was a successful journey. Now we just need to find a place to store all this food."

Bari got off the boat and stretched her limbs, feeling the chill of the early morning air. "What happened while I was asleep?" she asked.

"Nothing much," Alvin replied. "We had a smooth ride back, with the river's flow in our favour. We just docked a few minutes ago."

Elegast who had been waiting for their return since they left approached the group, carrying a large bundle of rope. "I'll secure the boat and start unloading the food," he said.

"Good idea," Alberad said. "Everyone else, let's go find a place to store the food. We need to keep it dry and protected from the elements."

The group made their way to a storage shed near the riverbank, where they spent the next hour unloading and stacking the food. When they were finished, they were all exhausted but satisfied with their work.

"Well, that's one task done," Cutter said, wiping sweat from his forehead. "Now we just need to wait for Nozos to come through on his end of the deal."

"I have no doubt that he will," Alberad said. "Now, let's go get some rest. We've earned it."

The group made their way back to their homes in Earnoche, each lost in their own thoughts. Bari was still wondering about the strange figures she had seen, but she pushed the thought to the back of her mind as she thought it was a dream. For now, she was just glad to be home and to have a well-deserved rest.

Chapter 41

A Heroes Welcoming

Gobulir, Ash, and Kalt finally arrived at the desert after their adventure in Postis. They were excited about their new-found wealth and eager to get back home to show it off. However, their excitement quickly faded as they realized the weight of the bags filled with gems was too much to bear.

"I think we should leave some of these jewels here and split the rest up," Kalt said as he struggled to drag the bag on the ground.

Gobulir quickly disagreed. "No way! Pick it up and carry on. We worked hard for this and we're not leaving any of it behind."

Ash interjected, "Gobulir's right, we need to keep going. We can rest when we get back to Cravmod."

Kalt grumbled but picked up the bag and they continued their journey. Despite the weight, they pushed on, determined to make it back to their village.

As they walked, Gobulir said, "You know, when we get back, we're going to be the talk of the town. Everyone will be envious of our wealth and all the adventures we've been on."

Ash smiled, "I can't wait to see the look on my mother's face when she sees all these gems. She's going to be so proud of us."

Kalt replied, "And think of everything we can buy with this wealth. We'll never have to worry about anything again."

The three friends continued their journey, chatting about their future plans for the gems. Despite the weight of the bags, their excitement for the future kept them going until they finally arrived back home, ready to show off their wealth and share their tales of adventure.

Gobulir walked into the main hall of Cravmod with swagger, a huge grin spread across his face as he held a bag filled with gems tightly in his arms. Ash and Kalt followed close behind, also looking pleased with themselves.

As Gobulir approached Brarmuk, he swung the bag around and said, "Look what we got!"

Brarmuk's eyes widened as he looked at the bag. "What's this?" he asked.

"These are the finest jewels that we took from the Aquanauts," Gobulir replied with a smirk.

Brarmuk's expression changed in an instant. He slammed his hand down on a nearby table, causing Gobulir and the others to jump. "You fools!" he shouted. "What were you thinking?"

Ash and Kalt looked at each other, confused. "We thought it would be a good idea," Ash said hesitantly.

Brarmuk ran his hands through his hair, clearly agitated. "You can't just take things from the Aquanauts. They are powerful and will not hesitate to retaliate."

Gobulir responded straight away "No they're ours now and they won't mind."

Brarmuk getting angrier with every word Gobulir was saying, replied "Return the jewels or be gone from Cravmod for good! We do not need enemies."

Gobulir, Ash and Kalt looked at each other, suddenly realizing the gravity of the situation. Brarmuk continued, "You need to take these back to the Aquanauts immediately and apologize for what you have done. I shall come with you to ensure it's done."

The sun had just risen, casting its warm light over the Cravmod kingdom. Gobulir, Ash, and Kalt found themselves being woken by Brarmuk. Brarmuk's eyes were stern and his voice was filled with urgency. "We leave now," he said, "We must return these jewels to the Aquanauts."

The three of them all uniformly agreed, still feeling guilty about the previous night's events. They had taken the jewels without permission and they knew they needed to make things right. However, Gobulir was visibly still annoyed that they had to return them. They gathered their things and set off, following Brarmuk into the harsh desert that lay ahead.

The journey was gruelling and the heat was intense. Gobulir, Ash and Kalt found themselves struggling to keep up with Brarmuk's pace, but they refused to give up. The sun beat down on their backs as they trudged through the sand, and the bags of jewels grew heavier with each passing moment.

At one point, Kalt stumbled and let out a groan, "These bags are too heavy," he said, "Can we leave some jewels here and split the rest."

"Not this again" Ash said.

"I think that might be a good idea" Gobulir said in agreement with Kalt.

Brarmuk's voice was stern as he interrupted, "We will not leave a single jewel behind. You must pick it up and carry on."

Gobulir, Ash, and Kalt knew they couldn't argue with Brarmuk. They picked themselves up and continued on, their determination fuelled by their leader's unwavering resolve.

Finally, after days of traveling, they reached Postis, the city of the Aquanauts. Brarmuk led the way, marching confidently through the streets until they reached the main hall. There, he approached Triton and Zale and offered them the bags of jewels.

"These belong to you," Brarmuk said, "We took them without your knowledge and we are deeply sorry."

Triton and Zale looked at each other, and then back at Brarmuk. They took the bags of jewels and, after a moment of consideration, Triton spoke. "Your honesty and willingness to make things right is admirable," he said. Zale then continued looking straight at Gobulir "But we already knew."

Brarmuk looking confused about the situation turned to Gobulir and said "What are they talking about?"

Before Gobulir could speak Naia stepped forward from behind Zale "He attacked me!" pointing directly at Gobulir.

Gobulir stepped forward and approached Naia, bowing his head in apology. "I'm sorry for what happened. I shouldn't have pushed you in the water, and I shouldn't have taken the jewels," he said.

Triton's expression was stern. "You may apologize, but your actions still have consequences. We need to make things right," he said.

Brarmuk stepped forward. "We are willing to make things right. What do you demand in return?" he asked.

Triton looked at the group, his eyes narrowing. "I demand the weapons you all have on you," he said.

Zale whispering to Triton "They look strong."

Brarmuk concurred, and he and the others handed over their weapons to Triton. "We accept this deal, now we must go and leave you in peace" Brarmuk said.

But just as they were about to leave Postis, Zale, spoke up. "This doesn't make us friends," he said holding some of the weapons in the air.

Brarmuk said "I understand. We just want to make things right and ensure that there are no further incidents," he said, before the group turned and left.

As they made their way back to Cravmod, Gobulir couldn't help but feel a sense of relief that the situation had been resolved peacefully. He just hoped that their actions wouldn't come back to haunt them in the future.

Chapter 42

Every Cloud Has A Silver Lining

The council chamber was filled with the Wyvinites, huddled together in a tight group. They were all looking up at the large clearings that showed the sky outside. The sun was shining, but a storm was brewing on the horizon. The wind was picking up and the sky was turning a dark shade of grey.

Shegilth, one of the youngest of the Wyvinites, stepped forward and asked Nozos, "Should we be scared of the storm that is coming?"

Nozos replied with a look of arrogance, "Not at all. The Wyvinites are not scared of any storm, no matter how big it may be." He looked around the room, making eye contact with each person, trying to inspire confidence. "We are strong and resilient, and we have faced many challenges before. This storm is no different."

But as he spoke, Aetire, one of the Wyvinites, whispered under his breath, "Maybe the storm is a punishment for giving away loads of our food to the Elvians."

Nozos heard the whisper and asked, "What was that? What was said?"

Aetire froze, not daring to look at Nozos. The other Wyvinites also grew quiet, not wanting to draw attention to themselves.

Nozos sighed, "Well, it doesn't matter. There's nothing to worry about. We Wyvinites are strong and will withstand any storm that comes our way."

The other Wyvinites all agreed, taking comfort in Nozos' words. They had faced many challenges before, and they always came out on top.

The Wyvinites were watching nervously as the weather outside started to take a turn for the worst. The thunder was getting louder and more intense, each crash echoing through the room. Shegilth couldn't help but get scared at this point.

As the storm got closer and closer, they could all feel the tension in the room rising. Suddenly, a bolt of lightning hit the volcano big pile of rocks flying around smashing the ground and lava started to spill out, quickly making its way down the mountain towards their remaining crops.

Nozos and Qyvrag both realised there was nothing they could do to stop the lava from destroying their crops, the lava was too fast and too hot. They all watched in despair as the fast-flowing lava quickly approached their fields, engulfing everything in its path.

"This is it," Nozos said, his voice filled with resignation. "We've lost everything."

The Wyvinites were silent, watching in horror as their crops were destroyed before their very eyes. The storm raged on outside, the thunder and lightning providing a backdrop to their sadness and despair.

As the storm began to clear, the Wyvinites looked out at the destruction left in its wake. The once lush fields were now blackened and burned, with the crops destroyed by the lava. Nozos and Qyvrag walked through the fields, surveying the damage.

"This is a disaster," Nozos said, his voice heavy with sadness. "All of our crops, gone in a matter of minutes."

"What will we do now?" Qyvrag asked, looking around at the devastation. "We have already given away so much food to the Elvians. How will we survive now?"

"We will have to start from scratch," Nozos replied. "We will have to replant and hope that the next harvest is better. But first, we must clear the fields and see what is salvageable."

The Wyvinites started to walk around, surveying the damage and starting to clean up. Some were crying, others were in shock.

As they worked to clear the fields, they were silent, each lost in their own thoughts. The once lively community was now filled with sadness and despair, a stark contrast to the mood just a few hours before.

"We will rebuild," Nozos said, speaking to everyone. "And we will come back stronger."

There were nods and murmurs of agreement from the others, but their eyes were still fixed on the ruined fields, a constant reminder of the devastation the storm had caused.

Bivis cautiously walked through the charred remains of what once were lush crops. He ran his fingers over the ash-covered soil, feeling for any signs of hope. As he approached Nozos, he could see the worry on his face, the storm had not only taken their crops, but also their future.

"Nozos," Bivis began, "it's not all bad news."

Nozos looked up, hope in his eyes. "What do you mean?" he asked.

"The storm may have been devastating," Bivis continued, "but it has also brought new opportunities. This ash will be a valuable fertilizer for our new crops, and the rocks that have been thrown out of the volcano will be a valuable resource for construction."

Nozos was shocked. He had never thought of it that way. He was used to seeing only the negative in a situation. Bivis, on the other hand, had always been a positive person. He saw the potential for growth and renewal in every situation.

"You're right," Nozos said, "we can start rebuilding and replanting. We can make this work for us, we can start anew."

Bivis replied, "There's more, I've been preparing for something like this. I built a pantry and stored food, enough for us to survive until the new crops grow."

Nozos's eyes widened in surprise. "Really?" he asked.

Bivis responded with confidence. "Yes, I had a feeling that something like this might happen. I wanted to be prepared."

Nozos was speechless for a moment. Then he said, "Bivis, this is fantastic news. I can't thank you enough."

Bivis smiled. "It's my pleasure. I just want to help in any way I can."

As the two of them spoke, the others started to gather around them, listening in on their conversation.

"What's going on?" Qyvrag asked, joining the group.

Nozos turned to face Qyvrag and the others. "Bivis has a pantry full of food that will last us until the new crops grow," he announced.

They all erupted in cheers and applause, grateful for Bivis's foresight and preparation.

Shegilth approached Bivis with a smile on her face. "Thank you, Bivis," she said. "You've saved us all."

Bivis blushed at the praise. "I just did what I could," he replied modestly.

Nozos put a hand on Bivis's shoulder. "Still, we are all grateful," he said.

And with that, the Wyvinites started to make their way back to their homes, their spirits lifted by the news of the pantry and the prospect of food to come. Despite the destruction caused by the storm, they were determined to rebuild and start anew, grateful for the kindness and foresight of one of their own.

"Thank you, Bivis," Nozos said, "for always finding the silver lining. We will rebuild, and we will prosper."

"Obsidian" Bivis said impatiently, still wanting to get more information across to Nozos.

"Huh?" Nozos and Qyvrag said at the same time.

Bivis approaches Nozos, and says, "There's more." Nozos raises his eyebrow, intrigued by what Bivis has to say.

"The rocks that were thrown out, they're obsidian," Bivis explained. "I've studied the properties of this material for a while now, and I think it could be used for armour. It's extremely durable and could protect us in battle."

Nozos and Qyvrag exchange a look, impressed by Bivis' knowledge and foresight. "We're grateful for your help, Bivis," Nozos says. "But armour isn't our priority right now. We need to focus on ensuring our survival and growing new crops."

Qyvrag intervenes. "We appreciate your concern, but we can handle ourselves in battle."

Bivis dipped his head, understanding their perspective. "I understand," he says. "I just wanted to offer my help in any way I could. If you ever change your mind about the obsidian, let me know."

Chapter 43

What A Wonderful Sight

The Elvians, Mountaineers, Aquanauts and Wyvinites were going about their daily activities. The Wyvinites were flying in the air, the Elvians were tending to their trees, the Mountaineers were working on their forges, and the Aquanauts were diving for pearls in the ocean. When suddenly, a high-pitched noise echoed throughout the area, nearly deafening everyone, they all clasped their ears and winced their faces.

As the noise grew louder, a massive gust of wind swept across the land, making everything sway and trees bend. Then, just as suddenly as it started, the wind and noise stopped, leaving an eerie silence in its wake. The sound of a pin dropping could be heard in the stillness.

Suddenly, the high-pitched noise started again, accompanied by a roar. Everyone looked towards the ocean, where a giant creature had emerged. It was Kraken, the giant sea monster that lived in the oceans depths. Kraken was a massive creature, towering in the air over the ocean water, with massive tentacles and a wide maw filled with sharp teeth.

Kraken roared again, and then quickly dived back into the ocean, leaving the area and moving on to the next, repeating the process. They all stood in awe, their eyes fixed on the spot where Kraken had disappeared. Some of them were stunned, others were frightened, and a few were in wonderment of the powerful creature.

As the minutes passed, they all continued to look out towards the ocean, waiting for any sign of Kraken. The anticipation was palpable, everyone was on edge, unsure of what was happening and why.

Chapter 44

The Elvians Despair

The Elvians were in a state of panic as they ran back to the centre of Earnoche. They had just witnessed a massive and powerful creature. They had never seen anything like it before and the thought of such a creature roaming the waters was terrifying.

As they arrived back to the centre of Earnoche, Alberad called for everyone to gather. The Elvians rushed to the main hall of Earnoche, their faces filled with fear and uncertainty. Alberad stood at the front of the hall, his voice echoing throughout the room as he spoke.

"Everyone, please calm down. We have seen something that we have never seen before, but we must not let our fear control us. We must act quickly and rationally to ensure our safety."

The Elvians all agreed in unity, their fear slowly starting to dissipate.

"I have called everyone here to discuss what we have just witnessed. Did anyone else see the creature? Does anyone know what it was?" Alberad asked, looking around the room.

Several Elvians stepped forward and spoke up, telling Alberad what they had seen.

Just then, Bari stepped forward, holding the Ancient book of Magic in her hands. "I know what it was," she said. "It was Kraken, and there is a story about this monster named Kraken. According to this book, Kraken re-emerges every three thousand years, causing destruction and chaos wherever it goes."

The hall fell silent as everyone listened intently to Bari's words. Alberad frowned, "What can we do to stop it?" he asked.

"According to the book, there is a way to defeat Kraken," Bari said, her voice growing more confident. "A powerful spell must be cast by a group of four chosen ones, one from each race that walks the land. They must work together to banish Kraken."

"Who are these chosen ones," Alberad said, determination in his voice."

Bari sceptically started "It says here the four chosen ones will reveal themselves at the time they are needed the most."

"We must act fast, my friends," Alberad said, bringing the room back to order. "We do not have much time. The fate of our land rests in our hands."

Chapter 45

The Aquanauts Alarm

The Aquanauts were in a state of panic as they raced around Postis. Everywhere you looked, people were talking, gesturing and shouting, trying to make sense of what they had just witnessed. In the midst of the chaos, Zale and Triton stood calmly, trying to ease the fears of those around them.

"Everyone, please calm down," Zale said, his voice ringing out over the din. "We don't know what just happened, but panicking won't help. Let's all gather together and figure this out."

Naia, Nixie, Ari and Roka huddled together in a corner, talking nervously amongst themselves.

"What do you think it was?" Naia asked, her eyes wide with wonder.

"I don't know, but I've never seen anything like it before," Nixie replied, still trying to make sense of what she had just seen.

"Do you think it was a monster?" Ari asked, fear creeping into his voice.

"It had to be," Roka said, her voice shaking. "Nothing else could make that kind of noise."

As they continued to speculate, Zale and Triton approached them, trying to bring some order to the situation.

"Everyone, please," Triton said, his voice firm. "We don't know what it was yet, but panicking won't help us find out."

"Triton's right," Zale said, nodding. "Let's all try to stay calm and figure out what just happened."

With that, they all gathered together, trying to make sense of what had just occurred and what it could mean for their community.

"I told you I saw something in the water," Toru said, he voiced in anger stepping towards the group. "I knew I wasn't seeing things. The monster you just saw was Kraken."

Triton approached Toru and asked him if he was sure that was the same monster that he saw. Toru stood firm, his eyes never leaving Triton's. "I'm positive," Toru said.

"So the ancient prophecies are true," Ari said. "They talk about Kraken destroys everything and everyone. And now, here it is."

Triton a determined look on his face. "We need to gather everyone and start preparing for whatever Kraken's arrival means. We need to be ready for anything."

Chapter 46

The Mountaineers Dread

As the Mountaineers heard the loud noises and roars that echoed throughout the valley. They all looked up to see a massive, beastly figure gliding through the desert, waving sand into the air as it went.

"What in the world is that?" Maldreg said, pointing towards the monster.

"It must be a dragon," Manaec said, with a hint of awe in his voice.

The group of mountaineers watched in awe as the monster disappeared into the distance. Just after it disappeared a sudden gust of wind hit them, carrying sand from the desert. They covered their faces and closed their eyes, trying to protect themselves from the sandstorm.

"What was that?" Brarmuk asked, brushing the sand from his clothes.

"It must have been from the monster," Maldreg said.

They all made their way back to the Mountaineer's hall, eager to tell the others about what they had seen and experienced.

Once they arrived at the hall, they immediately gathered around a large table and started discussing what they had witnessed. Some mountaineers were sceptical, while others were convinced that what they saw was real.

"I saw it with my own eyes," one mountaineer said, "It was a monster, I'm sure of it."

"But what kind of monster could it be?" another mountaineer asked.

Norakor cut into the conversation.

"That was Kraken," he declared with certainty but no one seemed to hear. "That was Kraken!" He shouted this time.

The group was taken aback. "Haven't I told you the story of Kraken many times before?" They all turned to look at him, waiting for an explanation.

Showing a page from an old book, titled Kraken. Showing a picture of Kraken towering over a group of four people "Kraken is a monster from the ancient times, it only emerges once every few thousand years," Norakor began. "It causes chaos and destruction wherever it goes."

Brarmuk stepped forward. "Well, let's get to work then," he said with a smile on his face.

The rest of the Mountaineers cheered in agreement. They were a proud and resilient people, and they were not going to let a monster like Kraken scare them.

Norakor clapped Brarmuk on the back. "That's the spirit," he said.

"We'll show Kraken what it means to mess with the Mountaineers," Brarmuk declared with a grin.

Chapter 47

The Wyvinites Concern

As the Wyvinites watched and heard the beastly roar of Kraken, Nozos' heart raced with both fear and excitement. He had never seen anything like it before and knew that whatever was coming was going to be a challenge for their kind.

"Zerig, Qyvrag, did you see that?" Nozos exclaimed, trying to keep his voice calm.

"Yes, we did." Zerig replied, his eyes never leaving the sight of the disappearing beast.

"What do you think it was?" Qyvrag asked, also trying to make sense of what they had just witnessed.

"I think it was what the Elvians were talking about," Nozos said, "Kraken."

Zerig and Qyvrag sighed in sync, their faces reflecting the fear and uncertainty that Nozos felt. But Nozos knew that he had to be strong for his people, and he stood tall, his wings spread wide, ready to face whatever was coming.

"There is no one stronger than us, my friends and family," Nozos declared, trying to reassure them who were now looking to him for guidance. "We are the Wyvinites, the protectors of this land. We will face this challenge head on, together if it comes to it."

They all agreed, their faces now determined as they all rallied behind Nozos. They knew that they were going to have to be strong, to work together, and to fight to protect their home.

"Let us prepare for battle," Nozos declared, you could see the Wyvinites had a fire brewing in their chests, ready for whatever Kraken had in store for them.

Chapter 48

The Discussion in Earnoche

Alberad gathered Cutter, Bari, and Keijo, his most trusted in the main hall of Earnoche. They were gazing at the large map of their region on the wall in front of them. The presence of Kraken had sparked a sense of urgency within all of them, and they needed to come up with a plan to defend their home and defeat the beast.

Alberad turned to the others, his deep voice echoing throughout the hall. "We must act quickly and come up with a plan to defend our home and defeat Kraken."

Cutter, his hand resting on the top of his axe said, "Indeed. We cannot let this monster wreak havoc on our land. We must protect our people."

Bari stepped forward, holding the ancient book of magic in her hand. "There is also mention of a powerful spell that can be used to defeat him. We will need the combined strength of all four races in order to defeat Kraken. We must all come together and fight as one."

Alberad, his expression concerned. "How will we let the other three races know of this spell?"

Bari turned to Alberad. "I will work on the spell to defeat Kraken. I'll act quickly, before it is too late."

Alberad stood in front of Cutter, Bari, and Keijo, in the main hall of Earnoche. The Elvians were known for their exceptional archery skills, but with Kraken's arrival, they needed to be better equipped. Alberad had a plan.

"We must create better weapons than what we already have to defend ourselves," Alberad began. "Elegast, our woodworker, has the skill to create the finest oak bows, but we need him to make them stronger, more powerful."

Cutter asked, "Elegast is a master woodworker, just look at the boat he crafted, but do you think he will be able to make such a powerful bow in time?"

"I'm sure he will," replied Alberad confidently. "We also need to build a bridge that crosses the deadly river so that we can leave Earnoche safely if a battle begins. We would need to take the battle to Kraken, we do not want Kraken in our lands, and I do not want the Tree of Life to get damaged."

Cutter and Keijo approached Elegast, the master woodworker of Earnoche, with a dire request. The two Elvians were grave and serious in their demeanour, and Elegast could sense their urgency.

"Elegast, we need your help," Cutter said, his voice echoing through the forest. "As Kraken has emerged we need a powerful bow that can defend our people."

Elegast, understanding the gravity of the situation said. "I can create a bow that is stronger than any I have made before, but it will take time and skill. I will start working on it immediately."

"We don't have much time," Keijo added, her voice filled with concern. "The safety of our people and the Tree of Life depend on it."

Elegast eyes lighting up with determination. "I understand the importance of this task. I will make as many bows as I can, as fast as I can."

Cutter and Keijo exchanged a relieved look and thanked Elegast for his help. The master woodworker got to work, gathering the strongest and most flexible wood he could find.

Cutter and Keijo's next task was to gather enough Elvians to start gathering the materials they needed to build a bridge. They went to Albwin and Alvin their trusted friends and asked for their help.

"Albwin, Alvin, we need your help," Cutter said.

"What can we do for you?" Albwin asked.

"We need to gather wood and vines to build a bridge. Alberad wants us to be able to leave Earnoche safely if a battle starts," Keijo explained.

"Of course, we'll help," Alvin said, "Let's go gather the materials we need right away."

The four of them set out to gather the materials they needed for the bridge. They searched the dense green forest for strong and sturdy trees that could be used for the bridge's support beams. They also searched the forest floors for strong vines that could be used to weave the bridge together.

Once they had gathered enough materials, they returned to the main hall where they found Alberad and the rest of the Elvians waiting for them.

"Good work, Cutter, Keijo, Albwin, and Alvin," Alberad said, "Now let's get started on building the bridge."

The group of Elvians started to work on the bridge, cutting and shaping the trees into the right size and shape for the support beams. Sweat dripping of their heads from all the hard manual labour. They then used the vines to weave the beams together, creating a sturdy and strong foundation for the bridge.

As they worked, they talked and discussed the plan for defending Earnoche against Kraken. They knew that they would need to be ready for anything and that the bridge was just one part of their overall plan.

"We have to be strong and brave if we're going to defeat Kraken," Cutter said, "But with the oak bows that Elegast is making and this bridge, we'll be ready for anything."

"I couldn't agree more," Keijo said, "Let's keep working and make sure that Earnoche and its people are safe."

The Elvians continued to work on the bridge, using their skills and knowledge to create a sturdy and safe bridge that would help them in their fight against Kraken.

Bari left the group of Elvians working on the bridge and headed back to her home. She was determined to find a way to defeat Kraken and protect her people. She remembered the Ancient Book of Magic that she had been reading before and decided to take another look at it.

As she sat down at her table, she opened the book and started to read through the pages. She came across a spell called 'Out of Body Communication' and decided to try and cast it. She closed her eyes and concentrated, reciting the incantation from the book.

Suddenly, her mind was transported to a different place, a place where she could communicate with others that were anywhere, even places she had never been to. She saw Triton, Brarmuk and Nozos.

"Greetings, I am Bari of the Elvians. I have some important news to share with you," she began. "I have found a spell in the Ancient Book of Magic that could defeat Kraken, but we need your help to make it work."

"What do you need us to do?" asked Triton, his curiosity piqued.

"The spell requires one person from each of the four races to gather and cast a magic spell. We need the power, strength, magic and courage. The four individuals don't know it yet but they will make themselves known when the time is right" Bari explained.

"I am ready to do whatever it takes to defeat Kraken," said Nozos, his voice firm.

"We will be ready," echoed Brarmuk.

"Count the Aquanauts in," said Triton, determination in his voice.

"Good, then it's settled. We must all also prepare in the event the worst happens and the spell fails, be quick in your preparations." said Bari, before the vision faded and she was back in her home.

Chapter 49

Brarmuk's Contingency Plan

Brarmuk was a seasoned warrior, and he had faced many battles in his lifetime. But the appearance of Kraken had him on edge. He needed to come up with a backup plan in case the spell Bari was working on failed. He was walking through the busy corridors of Cravmod when a glint of light caught his eye. It reminded him of the diamond they had found and the jewel they were given.

He briskly made his way to Sadeck's workshop. When he entered the workshop, he found Sadeck surrounded by a group of apprentices, all working on different pieces of armour.

"Sadeck, I need to see the armour," Brarmuk said, his tone urgent.

Sadeck raised an eyebrow but quickly led Brarmuk to a secure room. As soon as the door opened, Brarmuk was mesmerised by the room full of unique looking armours. Each piece had a slight tinge of red in it, and he could feel the power radiating from them.

"What is this?" Brarmuk asked, his eyes wide with wonder.

"The jewel we were given, I broke it down and infused it into the armour," Sadeck explained. "It has great strength properties and so has made our new armour stronger and more durable than any other armour I have ever made."

Brarmuk ran his hand over the red tinged armour, feeling the power coursing through it. "This will be my backup plan," he said. "If the spell doesn't work, we will have this armour to protect us and defeat Kraken."

Sadeck nodded, "I have never seen anything like this before. It truly is a marvel. But there is not enough for everyone in Cravmod. I have something else for you Sir"

"What is it?" Brarmuk said excitedly.

Sadeck opened a drawer in a cabinet next to him and carefully handed the diamond piece of armour to Brarmuk, who was in awe of its beauty and strength. The armour had a slight glow to it as the light from the fire bounced off of it, giving it an otherworldly appearance.

"This piece right in the heart section is impenetrable," Sadeck declared pointing to the centre piece, with pride in his voice. "The diamond Manaec found has been used in this piece of armour. We only had enough for this one piece though, I've made it to your size Brarmuk."

Brarmuk examined the piece closely, turning it around to see every inch. He could feel the strength from it, and he couldn't help but feel a sense of confidence knowing that he would be protected in battle.

"This is truly amazing, Sadeck," Brarmuk said, turning to him. "I can feel its strength just by touching it."

"I'm glad you like it," Sadeck replied with a smile. "It took a lot of time and effort to create, but it was worth it. With this piece of armour, you'll be able to stand against any enemy, even Kraken."

"This will be a great asset in the upcoming battle," Brarmuk said, grinning. "I can't thank you enough for your hard work."

Sadeck waved a hand dismissively. "It's my pleasure. I just hope it will be enough to protect all of us."

Brarmuk thanked Sadeck and left the workshop, feeling more confident and prepared for what was to come. He knew that with this armour and the spell Bari was working on, they stood a chance against Kraken.

Brarmuk was walking through the corridors, deep in thought. He knew that the situation was dire and they needed to come together as a united force to defeat Kraken. He thought to himself, "We need to make amends with the Aquanauts. They are an important part of this team and we cannot afford to have any internal conflicts right now."

He made his way to Gobulir, Ash, and Kalt. "Gobulir, Ash, Kalt," Brarmuk said, "I have a task for you. I want you to take this bag of weapons and go to the Aquanauts. I want you to put our differences aside and work as a team. We cannot afford to be divided right now."

Gobulir was hesitant, "You want us to go….out there?! We've just seen Kraken! And he's attacked me before. Why should I risk my life for them?"

Brarmuk replied, "Because right now, we are all in this together. We need to come together as a team to defeat Kraken. That is the only way we will be successful."

Ash stepped forward, "I'll go. I'll make sure they understand our intentions are to work together."

Kalt puffed out his chest, "Count me in too."

Gobulir sighed, "Alright, I'll go as well. But I'm not going to be happy about it."

Brarmuk placed his hands on Gobulir's shoulders, "I understand your reservations, but this is for the greater good. I have faith in you."

The three of them took the bag of weapons and started to make their way to the Postis. They walked through the mountain, their thoughts consumed with the task at hand. They knew that this was an important step towards defeating Kraken and ensuring the safety of their home, Cravmod.

Chapter 50

Underwater Tactics

Triton made his way over to Zale's perch, situated just above the coral reef. The sound of the waves crashing against the rocks was a constant hum in the background. Triton had been deep in thought since Bari's magical appearance. They desperately needed a plan to defeat Kraken, but so far, nothing had come to mind.

"Zale, we need to come up with a plan," Triton said, urgency in his voice. "We only have a few of the Mountaineers weapons and it's not enough."

Zale agreed, his long silver hair flowing in the wind. "I've been thinking about the underwater cave and tunnel system we found," he said. "It could be useful for flanking Kraken."

Triton raised an eyebrow. "How so?"

"Well, if we could use the tunnels to get behind Kraken, we could attack from the rear. It would be a strategic advantage," Zale explained. "Plus, the tunnels would provide some protection from its attacks."

Triton grinned thoughtfully. "That's a good idea. But we'll need more weapons. What are we going to do about that?"

Zale smiled. "Don't worry, Triton. I have a plan. I've been talking to the Merfolk and he has agreed to help us. He has weapons made of coral that are sharp and durable. With them, I'm confident that we'll have enough to defeat Kraken."

Triton smiled, feeling a sense of relief wash over him. It was good to know that everyone was helping in this fight. "Let's get to work then," he said. "We'll gather the Aquanauts and start preparing for battle."

Just as they were finishing their conversation, they noticed three figures emerging from the water. Triton and Zale were both taken aback, unsure of who they were and what their intentions were. They watched as the figures took off their water suits, revealing themselves to be Gobulir, Ash, and Kalt.

Zale immediately felt a surge of anger at the sight of Gobulir, memories of their last encounter where he had pushed his wife running through his mind. However, before he could react, Gobulir stepped forward and spoke up. "We come in peace," he said, holding his hands up in a gesture of surrender.

Ash then stepped forward, holding a large bag. "We want to make amends," he said, "and have brought these weapons as a peace offering." Triton took the bag and was surprised to see it was filled with weapons, much more than they had received from the Mountaineers last time.

Triton looked up at the three members of the Mountaineers, gratitude in his eyes. "Thank you," he said, and offered his hand to Gobulir in a show of peace. Gobulir took it, and the two of them shook hands, sealing the newfound alliance between the Aquanauts and the Mountaineers.

As they all put aside their differences and worked together, Triton and Zale felt a glimmer of hope. They had a new ally in their fight against Kraken, and with their combined resources, they might just stand a chance against the powerful beast. The once-strained relationship between the two races had now become one of cooperation and mutual support, and they all knew that they would need to work together if they were going to defeat Kraken and protect their homes.

Chapter 51

The Council Chamber Gathering

Nozos stood in front of the council chamber sat on his throne, surrounded by all the Wyvinites. He had called them together to discuss Bari's message, and the news of the spell that was needed to defeat Kraken. The room was filled with excitement and anticipation as they waited for Nozos to begin.

"Wyvinites," Nozos began, "We have received word from Bari of the Elvians about a spell that is needed to defeat Kraken. One of us will have to cast this spell."

As soon as Nozos finished speaking, a wave of confusion swept through the room. Everyone started to talk at once, asking who would be the chosen one and what they would need to do.

Nozos raised his hand to calm the crowd. "I don't have the answer to those questions yet. We must work together until the chosen one presents themselves, but first, we need to prepare ourselves. We need to be ready for what may come."

Qyvrag stood up, "We do not need to prepare ourselves. We are Wyvinites, we are strong enough already."

Nozos turned to Qyvrag. "Qyvrag, you are a respected member of our council, but we must listen to what Bari is telling us. We need to be ready for anything."

Bivis, approached Nozos and Qyvrag nervously. "We must remember the obsidian," he said. "We should take it to the blacksmith Baldemar who lives on a small island just southeast of the volcano. He can create us obsidian armour."

Qyvrag scowled. "We do not need any obsidian armour!"

Nozos interrupted, "Bivis is right Qyvrag. We must do everything we can to prepare ourselves. I will send some of you to take the obsidian to Baldemar." Nozos pointing at people in the room, "We will make sure we are ready for anything."

The council chamber erupted into a frenzy of activity as they started to make preparations. Nozos watched as they all worked together, and he was proud to be a part of such a strong and united community.

As the council chamber emptied, Nozos turned to Bivis. "Thank you for reminding us of the obsidian. We must be ready for anything, and I will make sure that we are."

Bivis agreed, "We will stand together, Nozos, and we will defeat Kraken. The Wyvinites will not fall."

Chapter 52

Always Check

The Elvians had been working tirelessly for days to build the bridge and in the tropical forest weather it was tough. Cutter, Keijo and the rest of the group had all chipped in, hauling heavy logs, tying thick vines, and weaving the materials together to create a sturdy structure. They were all exhausted but proud of their accomplishment.

As they finished and all stepped back from their tools, to admire the bridge, Alberad approached. "It looks great, but we need to make sure it's strong and can withstand our weight," he said. "We need a group of volunteers to walk across to the other side and test it."

Albwin and Alvin whispered to each other, clearly not eager to be part of the testing group "I'm not doing that." But before they knew it, Alberad had selected a group of Elvians, including Albwin and Alvin, to walk across the bridge.

The group reluctantly approached the bridge, and as they took their first steps onto the bridge, the structure creaked and swayed. Albwin and Alvin were frozen with fear, but the other Elvians pressed on, putting their weight on the bridge and testing its strength.

Despite the initial creaking, the bridge held firm, and the group made it safely to the other side. They all cheered and breathed a sigh of relief, glad that their hard work had paid off.

"It's a good thing we tested it," said Albwin. "I wouldn't want to be crossing that bridge in a hurry if we hadn't."

"I know," replied Alvin. "But I'm glad we did it. We can now say that the bridge is strong and safe to use…..I hope"

The Elvians all smiled, proud of their accomplishment. They had built a bridge that would allow them to cross the river and continue their journey. They were one step closer to their goal.

Chapter 53

Forging For The Future

As the Wyvinites finished their final preparations for a potential battle with Kraken, Nozos made his way to Baldemar's forge to check on the obsidian armour.

"How is it coming along, Baldemar?" Nozos asked as he approached the forges.

"They're almost done, Nozos," Baldemar replied, wiping the sweat from his brow. "The obsidian is proving to be quite difficult to work with, but I've managed to craft a few sets of armour that should provide some protection against Kraken's attacks."

"Excellent," Nozos said, looking at the armour. It was dark and shiny, with a slight tinge of red from the heat of the forge. "What do you think of its strength?"

"This is unlike anything we've ever had, but it's not the strongest," Baldemar said, running his hand over the armour. "This armour will give us extra protection. It should be able to withstand some attacks."

Nozos, feeling relieved replied. "Good. We may have to use it soon."

"Are you ready for the battle, Nozos?" Baldemar asked, looking up at him.

"As ready as we'll ever be," Nozos replied. "We have to protect our people and defeat Kraken. We have to be strong and brave, no matter the cost."

Nozos stood outside Baldemar's forge, carefully cradling the obsidian armour in his arms. The armour was a work of art, unlike anything he had ever seen before. The obsidian shards had been expertly forged together to create a suit of armour that was both light and flexible. Nozos was filled with pride as he made his way back to the Council Chamber.

As he entered the chamber, Qyvrag turned to him, a look of surprise on his face. "Nozos, what have you got there?" he asked.

Nozos approached him, holding out the obsidian armour. "This is the armour I went to see Baldemar about," he said. "He has crafted a suit of armour made entirely of obsidian, to protect us in the upcoming battle."

Qyvrag reached out and took the armour from Nozos, examining it carefully. He ran his fingers over the shards, admiring the craftsmanship. "This is truly remarkable," he said. "Baldemar has outdone himself."

Nozos nodded. "Yes, he has. And with this armour, we will be ready for anything Kraken throws our way."

Chapter 54

Calm Before The Storm

The day was going like any other day in the land of Earnoche. The Elvians were busy tending to the trees, the Wyvinites were doing their training, the Aquanauts were swimming and exploring the depths of the ocean and corals, and the Mountaineers were out hunting for food on the mountain of Cravmod.

Suddenly, without warning, the wind stopped blowing, the waves in the ocean settled, and the whole world became still and silent. It felt as though time had stopped, and everyone froze in place, looking around in confusion and fear.

"What's going on?" Alberad asked his fellow Elvians, but nobody had an answer.

Triton and Zale, who were exploring a new cave system, stopped in their tracks as they felt the eerie stillness. "This isn't natural," Triton said, and Zale was in agreement.

Nozos, who was in the Council Chamber discussing the latest strategies with Qyvrag, noticed the sudden calmness outside. "Something isn't right," he muttered.

The Mountaineers, who were out in the mountains, stopped in their tracks, weapons at the ready. "Stay alert," Brarmuk warned his companions. "We don't know what's coming."

As the stillness lingered, the silence grew more and more uncomfortable. The birds had stopped singing, and the only sound was the gentle rustle of leaves in the windless air.

"This is too quiet," Norakor whispered to Manaec and Araghed as they scurried along the rocks on the trail they were on.

As the minutes passed by, the eerie silence and stillness became almost palpable. The Elvians were in the midst of their forest, preparing for the day's fruit picking, but they all stopped in their tracks as the stillness became even more pronounced. Suddenly, a flock of birds flew out of the trees at an incredible speed, startling the Elvians.

"What in the world?" exclaimed Albwin.

"I've never seen anything like this before," said Alvin, as he watched the birds disappear into the distance.

Meanwhile, the Aquanauts were diving deep underwater when the fish around them started swimming frantically in all directions, as if trying to escape from something.

"What's going on?" asked Toru, confused by the sudden commotion.

"I have no idea," replied Nixie, as she watched the fish swim away.

In Cravmod, the deer and wolves suddenly appeared in a frenzy, running away as fast as they could.

"What's spooked them?" wondered Maldreg aloud.

At the same time, the Wyvinites were gathered in their stronghold when they saw all of the animals in the surrounding area take off in a hurry.

"What's happening?" asked Qyvrag, alarmed by the sudden disturbance.

Nozos, who had been keeping an eye on the area, spoke up. "Keep your eyes peeled," he said with a serious tone.

Suddenly there was a flash of blinding white light, causing everyone to cover their eyes and stumble. As the light faded, they were met with a deafening screech that echoed throughout the land. The ground shook beneath their feet as a deep, rumbling roar filled the air.

"What was that?!" Triton shouted, trying to steady himself.

"I don't know," Zale replied, looking around in shock. "But it can't be good."

The Elvians were equally alarmed. "What in the name of the forest was that?" Alberad asked, his voice trembling.

Bivis, who had been observing the scene from a distance, flew over to join the Wyvinites. "Did you feel that?" he asked, his eyes wide with fear.

Nozos sighed grimly. "We need to find out what's happening," he said, determinedly.

As they all exchanged worried glances, the ground shook once again, more violently this time. Everyone stumbled and fell to the ground, struggling to keep their balance.

Brarmuk watched as three figures emerged from the desert, becoming clearer as they approached. He recognized Gobulir, Ash, and Kalt. However, as he saw them walking towards Cravmod, his attention was drawn to something in the distance.

He turned his gaze to the horizon and saw the massive form of Kraken leaping into the air, its tentacles flailing. The creature smashed back down onto the ground with a thunderous impact, causing the earth to shake beneath Brarmuk's feet. Then, without warning, the desert began to give way to the ocean as water surged from the ground and started to engulf the arid landscape.

Brarmuk was stunned by the suddenness of the transformation, but he didn't have time to dwell on it. He turned his attention back to the approaching trio and yelled out to them. "Runnnnnnnnn!"

The water is rushing towards Gobulir, Ash and Kalt, they start to run as fast as they can towards the mountain of Cravmod. Kraken's destructive force is making it difficult for them to find a safe path, but they keep running, avoiding the boulders, rocks and dirt thrown their way by Kraken.

Gobulir turned to Ash and Kalt, yelling over the noise of the destruction, "Hurry, we need to get to the mountain!"

Ash responded, "I know, but it's not going to be easy with all this chaos."

Kalt added, "We need to keep moving, we can't let the water catch us."

As they continue to run, the mountain of Cravmod seems to be getting closer and closer, but so does the water. Kraken's roars and destruction are growing louder and more intense. They can feel the ground shaking beneath their feet.

Gobulir turns to Ash and Kalt, "We need to keep going, we can make it!"

Finally, they reached the mountain and start to climb up. They can see the water slowly rising and covering the land behind them.

Kraken then leapt back into the water causing an explosion of water and disappeared. As the mountaineers stood on the peak of Cravmod, they gazed upon the newly formed land that had emerged from the aftermath of Kraken's devastating power. The land stretched out before them as far as the eye could see.

Brarmuk turned to the others and spoke, "I have never seen anything like this. Kraken has changed the very landscape of our world, within seconds!"

Kalt replied confused, "But what about the desert? What happened?"

Gobulir shook his head, "I fear the worst. The ocean has consumed everything, and with Kraken's power, the land is not likely to recover anytime soon."

As Kraken disappeared, the land was filled with chaos and destruction. The Elvians, the Wyvinites, and the Aquanauts were all affected in one way or another. Trees were uprooted, rocks were split in half, and the land was marred with deep crevices.

The Elvians were fast to assess the damage, as the once beautiful forest was now scarred with deep trenches and fallen trees. Alberad, who had been surveying the damage, noticed that the bridge they had worked so hard to build was still standing strong.

The Wyvinites were also dealing with the aftermath of Kraken's attack. The fire pits that they used for cooking and forging had been extinguished. Rocks were laying scattered everywhere reminding them of the power of Kraken.

The Aquanauts, who had always felt safe in the water, were surprised to find that Kraken had managed to disrupt their aquatic world as well. The oceans coral was now broken and disturbed, and the fish and other sea creatures were in a state of chaos.

Chapter 55

Ready, Aim, Fire

Triton stepped forward and said, "So it begins. Prepare for battle." The same statement echoes throughout the various regions, and every race mobilises to gather their armour and weapons.

As the different kingdoms prepare for battle, they all shared their concerns and strategies.

The Elvians quickly gathered their arrows, swords, and shields. Alberad stood before the group of Elvians, looking out at the landscape around them. The sky was dark, and the air was thick with the scent of smoke and fire. The sound of battle echoing in his head.

"My fellow Elvians," he began, "we have prepared for this day. We have trained, we have built defences, and we have strengthened our walls. But we must be prepared to leave quickly, if it comes to that."

The group murmured in agreement, and Alberad continued. "We have built a bridge that will allow us to cross the river quickly and escape to the other side. If we must leave, we must do so quickly and efficiently. Every moment will count."

Albwin, who had been standing nearby, spoke up. "But what about our home? What if we can't come back?"

Alberad looked at him with a solemn expression. "We will do everything we can to protect our home, but if we must leave, we will find a new home. Our people are strong, and we will survive."

The group looked at each other, a mixture of determination and fear on their faces. They knew that the battle ahead would be difficult, but they were ready to fight.

"We will fight for our home, for our families, and for our future," Alberad said, his voice strong and resolute. "We will stand together and face whatever comes our way. Are you with me?"

The group cheered in response, their spirits lifted by Alberad's words. They knew that they were facing a difficult battle, but they were ready to fight to protect what they held dear.

Alberad raised his bow and shouted, "For our people! For our land!"

The others follow suit, raising their weapons and adding their own battle cries.

While the Aquanauts prepared their harpoons, tridents, and nets. Triton stood before his fellow Aquanauts, his eyes scanning the gathered crowd of sea-faring warriors. His voice was strong and confident as he spoke.

"Brothers and sisters of the ocean, today we face a great threat. But I am not afraid, for I know that we are the Aquanauts, and we know these waters better than anyone. Even Kraken himself."

The sound of agreement rose from the crowd, and Triton's chest puffed with pride.

"Our preparations are complete. Our weapons are sharp, our minds are strong. We are ready to face Kraken, and we will emerge victorious. Do not fear, my friends, for the oceans are our home, and we will not let this monster destroy it."

A round of cheers and applaud greeted Triton's words, and he bows his head, pleased with the reaction.

The crowd erupted in cheers once more, and Triton raised his trident high in the air.

The Wyvinites retrieved their spears, and gathered their thoughts. Nozos stood in front of the Council Chamber wearing his obsidian armour. He looked imposing and formidable, and his followers were visibly impressed.

"We are the strongest most powerful in the world," Nozos said, his voice filled with confidence and his eyes seemingly possessed. "With this and our Armour, we are unbeatable. Nothing can stop us!"

All the Wyvinites shouted in agreement, and some of them eagerly started to put on their obsidian armour.

"We need to be prepared for anything," Nozos continued. "Kraken is powerful, but we are stronger. Let's show him what we're made of!"

Nozos turned to his fellow Wyvinites and said with ferociousness, his eyes blazing with determination, "We will be in the air. Our strength will weaken Kraken, and our obsidian armour will protect us."

"This is it," he said. "Let's go out there and show Kraken what we're made of!"

The mountaineers equipped their axes and shields. Brarmuk addressed the Mountaineers gathered in Cravmod, his voice steady and resolute. "Everyone, the time has come to defend our home. Kraken has threatened our existence and we will not stand idly by. Sadeck has provided us with special armour, some of the strongest armour known to our kind. We will use it to protect ourselves and defeat the enemy."

The Mountaineers nodded in agreement, donning their tinted jewelled armour and preparing for battle. Brarmuk led them in a series of war chants, strengthening their resolve and raising their morale. As they readied their weapons and prepared to march, Brarmuk continued to address his people.

"We have lived in Cravmod for thousands of years. This is our home, and we will not let it be taken from us. Kraken may be powerful, but we are stronger. We will fight with everything we have and protect our land, our families, and our way of life."

The Mountaineers roared in agreement, their voices echoing throughout the mountain range. They set off towards the battlefield, their armour shimmering in the sunlight.

As they marched, Brarmuk could feel the tension and excitement building among his people. They were ready to face Kraken and defend their home. He silently thanked Sadeck for providing them with such powerful armour and prayed that it would be enough to protect them in the coming battle.

"We will be victorious," Brarmuk declared, his voice ringing out across the mountains. "We will not let Kraken destroy us. We are Mountaineers, and we will fight with everything we have."

The Mountaineers continued their march, their hearts filled with determination and a fierce sense of loyalty to their home. They were ready to face whatever came their way and emerge victorious.

As the different kingdoms finished their preparations, they looked to the sky, anticipating Kraken's return. The air was tense with anticipation, and everyone was ready to fight for their homes and families.

Chapter 56

Fail To Prepare, Prepare To Fail

Alberad walked through the partially destroyed lush green forest, surrounded by the Elvians. They were discussing tactics for the upcoming battle against Kraken.

"So, we'll have our archers positioned on the trees, using their bows and arrows to attack from above," Alberad said, gesturing towards the Elvian archers. "Our foot soldiers will be positioned on the ground, ready to attack when Kraken approaches. And our mage, Bari, will be at the back, providing support and protection the best she can."

Cutter, agreed. "Yes, that sounds like a good plan. Our archers are the best in the land, and they can shoot with incredible accuracy from the trees. And Bari you are skilled, we believe in you."

Alberad smiled. "Excellent. We're all in this together, and we'll need to work together to defeat Kraken. But I have faith that we can do it."

They approached the clearing in the forest, Alberad turned to face the group. "Alright everyone, let's get ready. Arm yourselves, and remember our plan. We need to be quick and coordinated if we want to take down Kraken."

The Elvians all had a determined look on their faces, and Alberad watched as they scattered to grab their weapons, gear and got in position. He couldn't help but feel a sense of admiration for these people, with their grace and prowess in battle. They would be a valuable asset in the fight against Kraken.

As the group began to get into formation, Alberad took a deep breath and prepared himself for the battle to come.

As the last of the Elvians were getting into position, a horde of lizard monsters suddenly emerged from the forest and charged towards them. The monsters had seemingly come out of nowhere and caught the Elvians off guard. Alberad shouted out to his warriors, "Attack! Don't let them break our formation!" The archers started to fire their arrows, hitting the monsters with deadly accuracy. The Elvian Foot Soldiers charged forward.

The lizard monsters were outnumbered and outmatched by the Elvians, who fought with courage and determination.

After what seemed like a quick and easy battle, the last of the lizard monsters fled in fear towards the bridge that the Elvians had built. The Elvians pursued them, hoping to catch them before they could cross the bridge and escape, but as the last monster crossed the bridge, it looked back with an evil stare and dropped its fire torch onto the bridge.

The bridge quickly caught fire, and the Elvians were thrown into a panic as they tried to put the small fire out.

"Quick, we need water! Put the fire out!" Alberad shouted, trying to rally his troops.

Some of the Elvians ran to the nearby stream and started to scoop water with their helmets and pour it onto the burning bridge. Others grabbed nearby tree branches and tried to beat out the flames and the rest were stamping out the flames with their feet..

Finally, after several tense minutes, they managed to put the fire out. The bridge was left badly damaged, but still intact enough for them to use.

"We can still use the bridge, but be careful," Alberad warned. "We don't know if they will try to attack it again."

As the Elvians were regrouping after the attack from the lizard monsters, Cutter noticed that T'Kal was missing from the group of monsters. He turned to Albwin and Alvin and said, "Did either of you see T'Kal with those creatures?"

Albwin shook his head, "No, I didn't see him."

Alvin furrowed his brow, "I didn't see him either. Where is he and what is he planning next!?"

Cutter's face turned serious, "I don't know. Hopefully we don't find out either."

Alberad, with his sword in hand, looked towards the horizon the other side of the bridge, where he could see the faint silhouette of Kraken. "This is only the beginning," he muttered under his breath.

Chapter 57

So It Begins

The mountaineers, Elvians, Wyvinites, and Aquanauts are all in position, waiting for the impending battle with Kraken. They stand in formation, each race with their own unique weapons and armour, but all united in their determination to protect their lands. They could all feel a palpable tension in the air. Everyone was nervously waiting for something to happen.

Suddenly, the ground begins to shake and the air grows thick with tension. The mountaineers look to the sky, while the Wyvinites scan the horizon. The Elvians listen intently for any sounds out of the ordinary, and the Aquanauts watch the waves for any signs of disturbance.

Suddenly, without warning, Kraken emerged from the ocean, soaring through the air and hovering over the battlefield. His massive form blots out the sun, casting an ominous shadow over its battlefield. The ground shakes beneath the feet of the warriors, and many of them are visibly shaking.

Fear was tattooed on the faces of every fighter. Most had heard stories of Kraken but not encountered, and nothing could prepare them for the sheer terror of being in his presence. Alberad is the first to break the silence, shouting out commands to his troops to hold their ground.

"Steady, everyone!" he cries out. "We can't let Kraken intimidate us. We've trained for this, and we will stand firm!"

But even as Alberad speaks, he can see the fear in the eyes of his people. Kraken is a force unlike any other, and they are all too aware of the danger they face.

Triton, who had been so confident just moments before, was now silent, his eyes glued to the massive creature hovering above them. "I...I didn't realise he was so big," he murmured, his voice shaking.

Nozos, standing tall in his obsidian armour, cried out to the Wyvinites, "We are the strongest warriors in this world! Kraken will not defeat us!"

Brarmuk, who had seen many battles in his life, was similarly stunned. "By the ancestors," he muttered under his breath. "I've never seen anything like this before."

As Kraken continued to hover in the air, the fear on everyone's faces only grew stronger, their eyes locked on the massive figure above. They gripped their weapons tightly, the sound of armour clattering against armour was the only noise. They all stand frozen, waiting for the inevitable attack.

As the tension mounted, the ground began to tremble ever so slightly. The vibrations were faint at first, but they soon grew stronger and more frequent. Ripples appeared on the surface of the water, and the trees began to shake and soon everyone could see the water rippling with increasing intensity.

For a moment, there was a tense standoff as Kraken simply waited. Then, suddenly, there was a loud roar from Kraken, and the vibrations and ripples intensified. The water began to churn and swirl. Suddenly, out of the water, tiny Krakens appeared, charging towards the armies with ferocious intent.

The ground shook with each of their steps. The Elvians in the forest trees began firing their arrows in a coordinated attack. The sound of arrows being loosed and the thudding of impact filled the air as the Elvians sought to stop the Krakens in their tracks.

Alberad shouted commands to his Elvians to prepare for the incoming onslaught. "Ready your swords! We must defend ourselves from these creatures!"

The Elvians continued to fire their arrows, but the mini Krakens proved to be fast and agile, making it difficult to hit them. As the creatures got closer, the archers switched to their swords and got ready to engage in close combat.

Keijo was knelt on her knees with her bow readied, she spotted a particularly large mini Kraken charging towards her. She took aim with her bow and loosed an arrow, but it missed its mark. With the Kraken almost upon her, she drew her sword and braced for impact.

Just as the Kraken was about to strike, it suddenly recoiled and fell to the ground. Keijo looked up to see Cutter charging towards her, wielding his sword with deadly precision.

"Thanks for the assist," Keijo said to Cutter as he joined her reaching out her hand.

Cutter said in response. "Don't mention it" whilst smiling and looking her in the eyes.

As the mini Krakens charged towards the Mountaineers, Brarmuk's voice echoed through the battlefield. "Charge!" he bellowed, and the Mountaineers ran towards the approaching creatures. The two sides collided in a ferocious clash, with the sound of metal clashing against the creatures and the roar of the Krakens filled the air.

Brarmuk led the charge, his diamond armour deflecting the blows from the Krakens' sharp claws. He swung his axe with all his might, crushing the mini Krakens that stood in his way. The other Mountaineers charged bravely alongside him, their new armour gleaming in the sunlight as they swung their axes and hammers.

"Stay together, don't let them flank us!" Brarmuk shouted, as he dodged another blow from a Kraken. The Mountaineers quickly adjusted their formation, keeping their shields up and their weapons at the ready. They fought back to back, their movements in perfect unison as they battled the Krakens.

"Watch out for their tails!" Maldreg yelled, as a Kraken whipped its long, spiked tail towards them. Maldreg quickly moved out of the way, but another Mountaineer was not so lucky. The tail hit him hard, knocking him to the ground.

The Aquanauts were taken by surprise as the mini Krakens swarmed towards them. They quickly realised that their usual tactics wouldn't work against such an overwhelming number of opponents.

"Triton, we need to regroup and come up with a new plan!" Zale yelled.

"I agree, but we don't have time for that now. We need to defend ourselves and protect our people," Triton replied, wielding his trident and blocking the first of the mini Krakens' attacks.

The battle began intense and as the Aquanauts struggled to fend off the relentless mini Krakens. They were outnumbered and outmatched, but they refused to give up.

"We need to keep them at bay, but we also need to find a way to take them out. Any ideas?" Triton asked.

"We could try to lure them into a trap. Maybe we can use some of our underwater mines to take out a group of them at once," Roka suggested.

"That could work. Let's see if we can draw them towards us and then set the jewel mines off," Triton agreed.

Triton, Zale and Roka made their way to where some of their underwater jewel mines were located followed by the creatures. Triton, Zale and Roka backed up slowly luring the mini Krakens into their trap. Bang! They had executed their plan and managed to take out a large group of mini Krakens with their jewel mines. But that was not enough, there were still more hoards coming, and the battle raged on.

"We can't keep this up forever. We need reinforcements," Triton said, as he fought off a few more mini Krakens.

The Wyvinites flew towards the mini Krakens as they got close, diving and grabbing them in mid-air. They landed with a roll, smashing the mini Krakens into the ground. The Wyvinites made quick work of them, snapping their necks and crushing their bodies. However, the mini Krakens quickly realised what was happening and started squirting water and black ink at the Wyvinites, blinding a couple of them. The blinded Wyvinites dropped to the ground, writhing in pain.

"Watch out for the ink!" shouted Aetire, trying to wipe the ink from his eyes. "They're squirting it everywhere!"

"We need to stay in the air and out of their reach," said Nozos. "We're vulnerable on the ground."

The Wyvinites took to the air, flying circles around the remaining mini Krakens. The mini Krakens continued to squirt ink at them, but the Wyvinites managed to avoid most of it. However, the ink made it difficult for them to see their targets, and they struggled to land hits on the agile mini Krakens.

"We need to take them out!" Qyvrag, dodging a stream of ink.

The Wyvinites began swooping in and attacking with deadly precision. With a few quick strikes, they managed to take out some the mini Krakens' eyes and tentacles, making them slow and vulnerable. They quickly dispatched the blinded creatures and flew back into the air, ready for the next wave of attackers.

"That was too close," said Zerig, wiping the ink from his obsidian armour. "We need to be more careful. Those mini Krakens are tougher than they look."

"Agreed," said Nozos. "We can't afford to underestimate them. We need to stay focused and be ready for anything."

The Wyvinites continued to fly, keeping a watchful eye on the skies for any more incoming mini Krakens. They knew that the battle was far from over, and that they needed to stay alert and ready for anything.

As the Wyvinites continued to dive towards the mini Krakens, they began to tire from the sustained flight. Their wings and armour were heavy and their breaths were laboured. Nevertheless, they pushed through the exhaustion and kept up the fight.

They continued to fight, their endurance being tested by the relentless onslaught of the mini Krakens. Their movements were becoming sluggish, and the Krakens seemed to be multiplying, making the fight more and more difficult. Despite their exhaustion, however, they refused to give up the fight. They were determined to protect their home and drive back the Krakens, no matter the cost.

Chapter 58

Time Of War

Cries of anger and fear mixed together as the battle raged on, with the Krakens seeming to come from every direction. The ground shook as they charged forward, and the air was thick with the sound of clanging weapons and shouting warriors.

Amidst the chaos, Brarmuk's voice rang out clear and strong, rallying the Mountaineers to fight back. "Don't give up! We are the Mountaineers! We will fight for our land and our people! Forward!"

Meanwhile, Kraken watched from the air, bellowing a deep, rumbling laugh that shook the very ground beneath them. It seemed as though there was no end to the number of mini Krakens it was summoning.

As the battle raged on, the air filled with smoke and dust, and the ground was littered with fallen warriors. But they stood strong, their eyes fixed on the swirling vortex of energy that marked the spot where Kraken hovered, knowing that they all needed this victory they just needed to hold out a little longer.

Brarmuk charged through the battle, his axe held high as he barrelled towards the approaching mini Krakens. Suddenly, a sharp pain pierced his chest, right where the diamond piece was embedded. He was thrown to the ground, momentarily dazed. The impact sent him flying backward, and he landed hard on the ground.

As he struggled to get back up and regain his composure, he groaned in pain, but he felt a sense of relief wash over him as he realised that the diamond piece had saved his life and saved him from serious injury. As he struggled to get back on his feet, he caught a glimpse of Sadeck grinning and winking at him from across the battlefield.

"Ha! I told you that armour was worth its weight in gold!" Sadeck said.

Brarmuk felt a sense of gratitude towards Sadeck. He knew that the diamond piece had saved his life, and he couldn't have done it without Sadeck's masterful engineering and craftsmanship. He looked at Sadeck with gratitude and said still slightly breathless from the impact. "Thank you, Sadeck. This armour is truly a life-saver." Brarmuk grit his teeth and marched forward.

"Let's finish this," Brarmuk growled, and charged forward once again towards the mini Krakens.

As Brarmuk marched forward towards Kraken, his eyes fixed on the creature, he suddenly felt a strong grip around his waist and chest. Looking down, he saw that one of Kraken's tentacles had wrapped around him, lifting him high in the air.

Brarmuk struggled against the grip, trying to free himself, but it was no use. The tentacle tightened its grip, crushing him in its grasp. He gasped for air as the pressure around his chest grew more intense, and then suddenly he was dropped to the ground with a deafening thud, spraying mud and dust in the air.

His fellow warriors rushed to his side, but Brarmuk was motionless, his eyes closed. Maldreg knelt beside him, his hand on Brarmuk's chest, feeling for a pulse.

"He's gone," Maldreg said, his voice choked with emotion.

The other mountaineers looked on in disbelief, their faces etched with sorrow and rage.

"We must avenge him," Reibeala said, her voice full of determination.

As they prepared to attack, a deep voice boomed through the clearing.

"Stop right there."

All heads turned to see Kraken hovering in the air, its massive body casting a shadow over the battlefield. The creature's many eyes glowed with a malevolent light as it spoke.

"You have caused me much annoyance, but I will give you one last chance to flee or surrender, and I will spare your lives."

"We will never surrender to you!" Maldreg shouted, his fists clenched in anger.

Kraken's eyes narrowed.

"Then you will all die," it said, and with that, it lashed out with its tentacles, sending a group of warriors flying in all directions.

The ground shook violently as Kraken's tentacles crushed everything in its path. The colossal creature still roared and thundered, destroying all in its path. Kraken slammed its massive tentacles onto the land, each one the size of a giant tree trunk. The ground shook violently, and rocks and debris flew everywhere. The races scattered, trying to avoid the massive tentacles and the destruction they brought.

The Wyvinites tried to fly away, but Kraken's tentacles reached up and grabbed them out of the sky, sending them crashing to the ground. The mountaineers tried to climb to higher ground, but Kraken's tentacles dislodged the mountains themselves, sending the mountaineers tumbling down.

Alberad tried to organize a counter-attack but the sight of the damage caused by Kraken made him falter. "What are we going to do now?" he yelled, feeling defeated. "We can't even touch him."

Triton, who had reappeared from the water, said. "We need to think outside the box" "We need to find a way to attack him from the inside."

Kraken continued its rampage, the land was destroyed. Trees were uprooted, buildings were demolished, massive waves crashed the shores and the ground was torn apart. The races could do nothing but watch in horror as their world was destroyed.

But before the Aquanauts could come up with a plan, something unexpected happened. Kraken started to shimmer, and then vanished without a trace the mini Krakens vanished along with it. The ground stopped shaking, and the sky cleared up, leaving the races bewildered and confused. All that was left was a devastated world.

"What just happened?" Toru asked, looking around.

"I don't know," Nixie said, scratching her head. "But I have a bad feeling about this."

Zale erplied "Me too."

The races looked at each other, wondering if Kraken would return, and if they were prepared for another attack. They knew that the battle was not over yet, and they would have to be ready for anything that came their way.

Chapter 59

The Effects Of War

As the dust and debris settle, the remaining members of the various races gathered to survey the devastation that Kraken had wrought upon their land. The destruction was catastrophic. Homes and buildings had been razed to the ground, trees uprooted, and the landscape was unrecognisable. The sky was a dark shade of grey, and the air was thick with the smell of smoke and burning wood.

Amid the chaos, they all noticed something different. New land had formed, and it looked different from everything they had seen before. A shimmering light emanated from the land, and it was surrounded by a ring of mountains.

As they gazed in wonder at the new land, they heard a rumbling noise, and the ground shook beneath their feet. They quickly realised that Kraken was still out there, and he was still dangerous.

Alberad, was one of the first to speak up. "We need to head towards the centre of that new land. We must investigate what has happened and figure out our next move."

The Elvians started making their way towards the new land. As they walked, they couldn't help but wonder what lay ahead of them.

"Perhaps this new land is a sign," suggested Albwin "A sign that we are meant to rebuild and start anew."

All the other races had similar plans, to make their way to the centre of this new unknown land as they had nothing left. Their homes had been destroyed, it was time for them to think of the next steps.

As they approached the new land, the groups were in awe of its beauty. The mountains surrounding the land were stunning, and the air was fresher than they could ever remember. The ground beneath their feet felt different, almost magical.

Triton, swam around the new waters of the land and reported back to the group. "The water around this land is teaming with new life. Plants and fish that we have never seen before. It's incredible."

The sky was turning a deep orange as the sun began to set, casting long shadows across the landscape. In the distance, each of the races noticed something strange, figures moving towards them that they didn't recognise. They quickly prepared themselves for the worst, their hands grasping their weapons, unsure of who or what was approaching.

The Elvians, perched high in the nearby trees, drew their bows and prepared to fire at the unknown figures. As they got closer, however, they realised the figures were the Wyvinites, and they lowered their bows in relief. "Ah, it's only the Wyvinites," Cutter said to his companions. "We can relax now."

Meanwhile, the Mountaineers, with their feet firmly planted on the ground, saw figures approaching from the sea. They were initially alarmed, but as the figures came closer, they saw that they were the Aquanauts. "Looks like it's just the Aquanauts," Reibeala said to the rest of the group. "No need to worry."

There was still concern however, for the two separate groups, as each group could see more unknown figures approaching each other.

As the two groups approached each other, they exchanged wary glances. The Wyvinites looked fierce with their sharp claws and scales, while the Aquanauts had weapons and armour made for underwater combat. Despite their differences, however, they approached each other with caution.

"Who are you, and what brings you here?" asked Alberad, his bow still drawn.

"We are the Aquanauts, and we are on a mission for Kraken," replied Triton stepping forward as he did so.

"And what about you?" asked Maldreg, eyeing the group of Wyvinites suspiciously.

"We are the Wyvinites, and we are here to kill Kraken who has destroyed our land," replied Nozos.

As they spoke, the tension began to ease, and they realised that they were not enemies but potential allies. They began to share stories of their travels and their missions, finding common ground despite their differences.

After a while, they realised that they had a common goal, to protect their world from any threats from Kraken. They decided to join forces and share information, pledging to help each other in times of need.

All four groups decided to stay together in the middle of the new land that had been formed. They started to set up camp and build shelters to protect themselves from the elements.

The Elvians climbed down from the trees and joined the other races on the ground. They used their knowledge of nature to gather materials for building and foraging for food. The Wyvinites flew high above the land, scouting for any potential threats or resources. The Mountaineers used their strength and endurance to gather large rocks and boulders to fortify their camp.

As the races worked together to build their new home, they began to share stories of their past and traditions. The Elvians talked about their deep connection to nature and their peaceful way of life. The Wyvinites spoke of their fierce warriors and their strong sense of honour. The Mountaineers shared their love for adventure and their ability to overcome any obstacle. And the Aquanauts told stories of the ocean and how they were masters in the water.

As the sun set on the new land, the races sat together around a large fire, enjoying a meal made from their combined efforts. They discussed plans for the future, including exploring the surrounding areas and discovering the secrets of the land.

Chapter 60

The Cold War

As the new day dawned, the races woke up from their well-deserved rest, stretching and yawning as they prepared to start the day. The smell of wood smoke drifted through the air as breakfast was being cooked, and the sound of laughter and chatter filled the air. The previous day's battle and the new land they found themselves in were still fresh in everyone's mind, but for now, they were just happy to be alive.

As they gathered supplies and started to eat breakfast, the air around them suddenly changed. A chill spread throughout the area, causing the hairs on the back of their necks to stand on end. It wasn't long before the first snowflakes started to fall from the sky, gently at first, and then rapidly increasing in intensity.

The Elvians, Mountaineers, Aquanauts, and Wyvinites all look up in amazement at the sudden snowfall. Some of them had never seen snow before, and others only experienced it in small doses. The white flakes continued to fall, covering the new land in a thick blanket of snow.

As they looked around at the unfamiliar landscape, they couldn't help but feel a sense of awe and wonder. The trees were adorned with frost, and the lakes and rivers were getting colder by the second. The entire world around them had been transformed into a winter wonderland.

The races quickly realised that they need to prepare for this new weather. The Aquanauts dove into the nearby lake, searching for fish that they could cook for their meals. The Elvians started to gather wood for fires and other materials to build shelter with, while the Wyvinites scouted the area for any potential dangers. The Mountaineers, on the other hand, started to dig into the snow to create a makeshift fortress.

The different races were going about their business, gathering supplies and enjoying the new land they had discovered. But suddenly, a loud rumbling noise shook the ground, and vibrations could be felt throughout the area.

The Elvians, Mountaineers, Aquanauts, and Wyvinites all looked at each other, wondering what was happening, and they all got to their feet in a panic. Suddenly, out of nowhere, Kraken and mini Krakens appeared, fast approaching them. They all immediately got into battle mode, grabbing their weapons and preparing for the worst.

The Elvians quickly took their positions in the trees, ready to fire their arrows at the incoming Krakens. The Mountaineers stood their ground, their axes and hammers at the ready, gritting their teeth. The Aquanauts quickly dove into the water, ready to defend themselves. The Wyvinites took to the air, flying high above the Krakens, ready to strike at any moment.

As the Krakens approached, the different races could see the anger and rage in their bulging eyes. The Elvians fired their arrows, and the Mountaineers charged forward. The Aquanauts launched themselves at the Krakens, using their tridents to strike. The Wyvinites dove down from the sky, their claws outstretched, ready to grab onto the Krakens.

Despite their best efforts, the Krakens were too powerful and too many. The Krakens were able to take out many of their enemies, leaving hundreds of bodies on the floor, lifeless. The Elvians had to retreat to higher branches in the trees to avoid the Krakens' attacks. The Mountaineers were flung high in the air by the Krakens' tentacles. The Aquanauts struggled in the water, unable to keep up with the Krakens' speed. The Wyvinites were getting tired, unable to keep flying for much longer.

Despite the odds, the different races refused to give up. Triton, knowing he had to do something and soon called out to his fellow water inhabitants, Zale and Roka, to follow him. He had spotted a hidden underwater cave system that seemed to be like the other they had encountered before. Zale and Roka gathered around Triton, their faces filled with curiosity and nervousness.

"Listen up, my friends," Triton announced. "I have discovered a new underwater cave system, and I think it could help us in this fight. I suggest we explore it and counter Kraken from behind."

Zale and Roka agreed without hesitation, and Triton led them towards the entrance of the cave system. However, their journey was soon interrupted by a group of mini Krakens, which began attacking them fiercely. The Aquanauts, well-prepared for such situations, quickly drew their coral weapons and fought back with all their might. Despite the fierce resistance put up by the mini Krakens, the Aquanauts managed to slaughter the mini Krakens leaving them gurgling in their black blood and continue their journey into the cave system.

As they ventured deeper into the cave, the Aquanauts marvelled at the beauty and wonder that surrounded them. The cave walls were covered in glowing underwater flora, and schools of colourful fish swam by their sides. They could sense something special was hidden deep inside this mysterious cave.

As they turned a corner suddenly, a group of larger Krakens appeared before them, blocking their path. The Aquanauts braced themselves for another fierce battle, but before they could react, the Krakens began to communicate with them telepathically.

"Put down your weapons now!" the Krakens spoke. "Bow down to our Master."

Zale's eyes widened in shock as the Krakens spoke to him and his fellow Aquanauts telepathically. He had never heard of such a thing before. Triton and Roka looked just as stunned.

The Krakens spoke of unjustifiable actions, Zale couldn't shake the feeling of unease. What if they were just going to kill them? Suddenly, a thought came to Zale's mind. He slowly reached down and unclipped a gem from his hip, feeling its weight in his hand.

Without a word, he launched the gem at the Krakens, and there was a loud explosion that echoed through the cave. Shards of gemstone flew in all directions, and the Krakens let out a screeching howl of pain as it hit them. Zale watched as they writhed in agony, wondering if he had just made a terrible mistake.

But then, to his amazement, the Krakens started to shrink and dissolve into the water. As they disappeared, Zale could hear their telepathic voices fading away.

Triton and Roka were staring at him in disbelief. "What was that?" Roka asked, still processing what had just happened.

"It was a gem grenade," Zale replied, trying to catch his breath.

Triton and Roka thanked Zale for his heroic actions and continued on their journey. They swam through the underwater cave system, following the light that was growing brighter and brighter as they approached. The trio was determined to find a way to defeat Kraken once and for all.

As they got closer, Triton noticed that the light coming from the exit would lead them behind Kraken. He signalled for Zale and Roka to slow down and they observed the massive creature from a distance. It was then that Triton noticed something peculiar about Kraken's movements.

"Look," he whispered to his companions, "Kraken's movements are becoming sluggish. It's as if it's weakened, injured or tired."

Roka smiled and said "Maybe. Zale got anymore of them gem grenades, they could do damage to Kraken."

Searching his waist Zale responded "It looks like I only have one left".

Triton quickly interrupted with a plan. "We need to get behind Kraken and take advantage of its weakened state. Let's move slowly and quietly, so as not to draw attention to ourselves."

They swam as silently as possible, making their way behind Kraken's massive body.

"We need to find a way to use this position to our advantage," Triton said, "but we can't do it alone. We need to get our allies attention."

Qyvrag, grew impatient as they had yet to defeat Kraken. He felt restless and eager for victory, believing that the Wyvinites were the strongest and most powerful race. Qyvrag roared in frustration, causing some of the other races to stop in their tracks.

Suddenly, he spotted a group of Krakens alone, and without a second thought, he launched himself at them, his sharp talons slicing through their flesh. Qyvrag let out a deafening battle cry as he continued to attack, his wings flapping furiously as he soared through the air.

As he landed on the ground, he continued to swing his massive tail, slamming it into the Krakens with each strike. The other races watched in awe as Qyvrag fought with incredible strength and ferocity, his scales glistening in the sun.

"Remember, we Wyvinites are the strongest! We will not be defeated!" Qyvrag shouted triumphantly as he stood amidst a pile of defeated Krakens. The other races looked at him with a mix of admiration and fear, not knowing how to react to his display of power.

But as Qyvrag surveyed the area, he noticed that the other Krakens were starting to close in on him, outnumbering him. Despite his bravery, he realised he might have gone too far. He quickly retreated back to the safety of his fellow Wyvinites, panting heavily from his exertions.

"Perhaps we should stick together and not underestimate the power of our enemies," Alberad spoke up, addressing Qyvrag and the other races. "We may have different strengths, but united, we can face any challenge."

Qyvrag, somewhat begrudgingly said. "Very well, but let it be known that our people are still the strongest!" he declared, puffing out his chest proudly.

The other races exchanged glances but didn't say anything, knowing that it was best not to provoke the fiery Wyvinite any further. As they continued their journey, they knew that they would have to work together to face whatever challenges lay ahead.

Chapter 61

We Are One

Meanwhile, Cutter's keen eyes spotted Triton creeping up behind Kraken, and he knew he had to act fast. He quickly called out to Keijo, Albwin, and Alvin, telling them to move forward with him. They all grabbed their bows and arrows, ready to take on the approaching Krakens.

"Come on, we have to push forward and help Triton," Cutter shouted as they advanced. "Stay alert, and keep firing at those Krakens."

Keijo, Albwin, and Alvin followed Cutter's lead, firing arrows at the Krakens that were closing in on them. The creatures were fast, but the small group's coordinated attacks kept them at bay.

"We have to hurry," Cutter yelled to the others. "Triton can't wait much longer."

With renewed vigour, the group pushed forward, firing arrows at the Krakens and cutting down any that got too close. As they neared Triton, gave them a nod of appreciation, grateful for the backup.

Maldreg was patrolling the battlefield when he spotted the group of Elvians moving forward. He noticed that they were being followed by a pack of Krakens, and he knew that they needed help. He quickly signalled to his fellow Mountaineers and they all moved in to help.

As they marched in, Maldreg saw Nozos, land on the ground and start moving forward on foot. Maldreg was surprised to see the Wyvinite out of the air, but he quickly realised that Nozos was a valuable ally.

Maldreg and his team of Mountaineers swooped down on the Krakens, swinging their axes down on them. Nozos, on foot, charged forward and used his wings and strength to create a barrier around the Elvians, protecting them from the Kraken attacks.

As they fought, Maldreg and Nozos shouted encouragement to each other, coordinating their attacks and movements. The Elvians, grateful for the help, fought bravely alongside them, their arrows finding their mark.

Maldreg saw a particularly large Kraken heading straight for Nozos. Without a seconds thought, he dove towards the Kraken, throwing his axe at the Kraken. The Kraken turned to face him, but it was too late. Maldreg's axe had engulfed the Kraken's face, and it fell to the ground, dead.

"Thank you for your help," said Cutter. "We couldn't do this without you."

Maldreg smiled. "We are all in this together," he said. "We must fight as one if we are to defeat Kraken and his minions."

Nozos agreed. "We may be different races, but we share a common goal," he said.

The group was huddled together, discussing their plan of action when suddenly, without warning, Kraken attacked. Its massive tentacles flailed through the air, striking out at anything in its path. Albwin, one of the Elvians, was caught in the fray and was thrown high into the air.

The group gasped in horror as Albwin's limp body collided with a nearby rock, his head hitting it with a sickening thud. They rushed to his side, but it was already clear that he was beyond help. The once vibrant and full of life Albwin now lay motionless on the ground, his eyes staring blankly into the white sky.

The group was filled with grief and anger at the sudden loss of their comrade. No one spoke for what felt like an eternity, the only sound being the distant echo of Kraken's bellowing roar and the clashing of weapons.

Finally, Maldreg broke the silence, his voice low and filled with sorrow. "We must avenge Albwin's death. We cannot let Kraken continue to terrorise this land."

The others all roared in agreement and frustration, their eyes blazing with determination. They knew that they had to fight back, no matter the cost. As they stood up, weapons at the ready, the group prepared themselves for one last push.

Kraken would pay for what it had done. And they would make sure that Albwin's death would not be in vain.

The group charged forward towards Kraken in the thick snow, their weapons at the ready. Triton, Roka and Zale saw the group and joined in the charge, Tritons trident poised with power. As they closed in on Kraken, suddenly Zerig, Toru, Reibeala, and Cutter started to illuminate with an intense bright white light. Everyone stopped and stared in confusion and awe, unsure of what was happening.

"What in the name of the sea is happening?" Triton shouted as he shielded his eyes from the bright light.

"I don't know, but it's happening to me," Zerig replied, looking down at his hands in amazement.

The light grew brighter and brighter, engulfing the four of them. Suddenly, the light fades, and the group found themselves surrounded by a shimmering aura. They feel a surge of power and energy coursing through their bodies.

"I feel stronger," Toru exclaimed, flexing his muscles.

"Me too," Cutter said with confidence, unsheathing his sword.

Reibeala spoke up with bemusement, "I feel as though I can take on anything."

Zerig looked around at the group, "We must have unlocked some kind of power within us. But what does it mean?"

As the group of adventurers glowed, Bari noticed the change from a distance. She had been keeping watch over the children while the others fought Kraken, hoping for their success. But when she saw the glow, she knew that the time had come to use the spell to defeat Kraken.

Without hesitation, she quickly gathered the children around her and cast a protective spell that created a large bubble around them. She could hear the rumbling of the ground and the sounds of the battle in the distance, but she focused all her energy on maintaining the protective bubble around the children.

As she ran steadily "By the power of earth and sea,
Let a shield surround us thee,
Protect us from all harm and strife,
As we navigate this dangerous life."
The children were confused and frightened, but Bari's calming presence kept them moving forward.

As Bari and the children got closer to the group, the glow intensified, and she knew that the spell had to be done as soon as possible before it was too late.

Bari was running as fast as she could towards the group, her heart racing with the hope that the spell would work. She knew that they were their only hope.

As Bari got closer to the group, she threw the ancient book at Cutter, who leaped into the and just about caught it with his fingertips. Cutter landed on the floor and automatically frantically searched through the book, his eyes darting back and forth across the pages, looking for the spell that would save them all.

As Cutter was searching for the spell Reibeala, Toru and Zerig start to back up towards Cutter, preparing for the inevitable, their weapons still at the ready.

"Come on, come on," Cutter muttered under his breath, his fingers moving quickly over the pages. "Where is it? It has to be here somewhere."

Bari watched as Cutter's face twisted with frustration and despair. She knew how much was at stake and how hard Cutter was trying to find the right spell.

Suddenly, Cutter's eyes widened and he let out a cry of triumph. "I found it! This is it!" he exclaimed, holding up the book for everyone to see.

Taking a deep breath, Cutter began to read the spell aloud. His voice grew louder and more powerful as he continued, and Reibeala, Toru, and Zerig joined in, their voices joined together to form a powerful chorus that echoed throughout the snow filled land. They kept their eyes locked on Kraken as they recited the words with unwavering determination.

"Let water and wind, earth and flame,
Rise up together and vanquish this Kraken's name.
By the force of our will and the strength of our hearts,
Let Kraken be defeated and torn apart.
May the ocean be free and the land be saved,
By the power of this spell, let Kraken be enslaved."

Suddenly, the mini Krakens surrounding them begin to dissolve into dust, causing the ground to shake as their bodies disintegrate. The dust swirls around Kraken, obscuring its form and causing it to thrash about in confusion.

The group repeated the incantation, their voices grew stronger with each passing moment.

"Let water and wind, earth and flame,
Rise up together and vanquish this Kraken's name.
By the force of our will and the strength of our hearts,
Let Kraken be defeated and torn apart.
May the ocean be free and the land be saved,
By the power of this spell, let Kraken be enslaved."

As they spoke the final words of the incantation, a bright light began to emanate from their hands and spread outward, encompassing the entire area. The light grew brighter and brighter, until it was almost blinding.

In the centre of the light, Kraken writhed and screamed, unable to resist the power of the spell. As the light faded away, Kraken fell to the ground, defeated and powerless.

Cutter, Reibeala, Toru, and Zerig breathed a collective sigh of relief, grateful for the successful spell. "We did it," Cutter exclaimed, "We defeated Kraken and saved the ocean the land and our people!"

The group cheered and hugged each other, relieved that the battle was finally over. They knew that the victory had only been possible through their teamwork and determination, and they were proud of what they had accomplished.

Chapter 62

At Last

As the dust settled and the group of heroes stood there in amazement, smiles and cheers spread across their faces. They had just defeated the powerful Kraken and saved their people. However, their joy was interrupted by Nozos.

"Hey! I wouldn't be so sure, someone should go check and make sure that Kraken is actually dead."

Everyone looked at each other nervously, but no one volunteered to go. Nozos impatiently stormed off towards Kraken's massive body, which lay motionless on the ground.

"I'll guess I'll go check then." He said looking at everyone else as if to make a point on how unfazed he was to go and check.

However, as Nozos approached Kraken, his heart raced with anxiety. He nervously checked Kraken's massive body, looking for any signs of life. After a few moments of tense inspection, Nozos finally let out a sigh of relief and confirmed that Kraken was indeed dead.

Nozos then rushed back to the group to deliver the good news.

"He's dead! Kraken is dead!" Nozos exclaimed, relief evident in his voice.

The group erupted into cheers and congratulated each other on their hard-won victory. They had finally defeated the Kraken and saved their people from certain destruction.

As the group celebrated their victory over Kraken, Gobulir rushed forward towards the fallen beast, clutching onto Ask and Kalt dragging them with him. His eagerness to examine the creature up close is met with a mix of amusement and concern from the rest of the group.

Maldreg chuckled and said, "Be careful there, Gobulir. We don't want you to become Kraken's next meal."

Gobulir grinned sarcastically back to Maldreg and responded, "Don't worry, Maldreg. I'm not afraid of a little danger."

As Gobulir approached Kraken, Gobulir's excitement grew massively. He moved closer and closer until he was standing right next to the massive creature's head. The stench of decay and seawater was overwhelming, but Gobulir was unfazed as he ran his hand over the beasts face.

As Gobulir ran his hands over Kraken's face, he felt something hard in its mouth. Curious, he took a closer look and saw that the Kraken's teeth were filled with what looked like sparkling diamonds and shimmering jewels.

Without thinking, Gobulir reached in and tried to pull out the diamonds and jewels but failed, they did not budge. He stood up, clutching Ash and Kalt in his arms and dragged them to the group not saying a word to them about what he had just seen. His heart was beating fast, he didn't want anyone to know what he had found, not yet anyway. As he reached the others, he carefully placed Ash and Kalt on the ground.

"What did you find?" Reibeala asked, her eyes fixed on Gobulir's hands.

Gobulir hesitated for a moment, and then shook his head. "Nothing," he said, trying to keep his voice steady. "Just a few scraps of Kraken's flesh."

Reibeala frowned, but didn't press the issue. Gobulir breathed a sigh of relief and tried to steady his breathing. He knew he had to be careful with what he had found.

Chapter 63

Devastating Affects

As the war came to an end, the group was left sitting in the aftermath by the crackling fire. The landscape around them was desolate, with the ground scorched and littered with debris. The bodies of fallen Krakens, Wyvinites, Elvians, Mountaineers and Aquanauts lay scattered throughout the area, their lifeless forms a grim reminder of the toll the war had taken on them all.

The group was silent as they took in the devastation around them. The once beautiful scenery was now nothing but a wasteland, and the air was thick with the smell of smoke and death. The sun had set, casting an eerie white glow from the moon over the landscape, as if even the sky was mourning the loss of life.

After a few moments of sombre silence, the group gathered solemnly on the edge of the now barren landscape. Albwin's body was carried to a nearby clearing where they could hold a proper funeral. As the Elvians laid him to rest, the group remembered all the times they had spent alongside him and the sacrifice he made for them, the wind rustled through the fallen trees, as if paying tribute to the fallen Elvian.

Keijo, her face etched with grief, stepped forward to speak. "Albwin was a brave and selfless Elvian," she began, her voice shaking slightly. "He fought with honour and died protecting his comrades. We will never forget his sacrifice."

Everyone gathered in the group to be a part of Albwin's funeral had tears streaming down their faces. Bari, standing off to the side with the children, clutched a small bouquet of wilted flowers tightly in her hand. She stepped forward and placed them on top of the Albwin's body, whispering a silent prayer.

Alberad, usually the speaker of the group, was uncharacteristically quiet. He stood off to the side, his head bowed in respect. Cutter, his usual confident demeanour was now replaced by sadness, stared at the ground, lost in thought.

As the group began to disperse, each lost in their own memories of Albwin, Keijo remained behind, kneeling at his body. "Rest in peace, my friend," she whispered, her voice choked with emotion. "Your bravery will never be forgotten."

The moon continued to glow overhead, and the stars twinkled above them. The group walked in silence, each lost in their own thoughts. As they reached the fire pit, Cutter turned to the others.

"We will continue as we always have," he said firmly. "We will honour his memory by marching on."

Qyvrag's voice interrupted Cutter as the group stood amidst the ruins that lay in front of them. "Don't be so positive," he said, his tone harsh and bitter. "Look around you. There's nothing left."

The entire group looked around at the devastation that surrounded them. Trees and mountains were reduced to rubble, and the once-lush meadows were nothing but barren wasteland. The group was silent, all thinking about the losses they had suffered during the war.

Toru was the first to speak, his voice barely above a whisper. "But we have each other," he said, looking around at the group. "We can rebuild. We can start over."

Qyvrag snorted. "And what about those who aren't here to start over?" he asked, his voice rising. "What about Albwin? He's dead, and he's not coming back."

Before Qyvrag could continue, Triton interrupted him and suggested that they should try to get some sleep.

"I think we should rest for a while," he said, "We can't do anything now, and we're all exhausted."

Qyvrag scowled at Triton's words but didn't say anything. He was clearly not happy with the situation, but he knew that Triton was right.

As the group started to settle down for the night, Cutter suggested that someone should stay awake to keep watch. "We should take turns keeping watch," he said. "We don't know what's out there, and we need to be careful."

Reibeala spoke up in agreement, "It's a good idea, Cutter. We need to be careful."

Gobulir, who was lying down with his head resting on a fallen tree at this point, shot upright and said, "I'll take the watch!"

The others all thanked Gobulir, and so Gobulir got up and walked a short distance away from the group, where he sat down on a rock and watched the area around them.

Chapter 64

What You Don't See Doesn't Hurt

As the night wore on, the group slept fitfully, their dreams filled with the horrors they had witnessed in the past few days. Gobulir remained awake, his eyes scanning the darkness for any sign of danger.

As Gobulir sat on a rock, looking out into the night. His mind was racing, and his heart was pounding. He couldn't stop thinking about the jewels he had seen in Kraken's mouth. He knew that they could be valuable, but he also knew that they could bring trouble. As he looked around, he saw that the rest of the group was asleep. He didn't want to wake them, but he also couldn't shake the feeling that he needed the jewels.

He got up and walked towards Kraken, taking care not to make any noise. As he approached and carefully pried open its mouth, he could see the diamonds and jewels shining in the moonlight. He couldn't believe his luck. He reached out to touch them, but hesitated. What if someone saw him? What if he woke someone up?

Gobulir looked back at the group and saw that they were still sound asleep. He let out a sigh of relief and turned back to the jewels. He reached into its mouth and tried to pry the first jewel loose, but it was wedged in tight. After a few failed attempts, Gobulir finally managed to wrench the jewel free with a loud pop. He let out a sigh of relief, but as he tried to retreat, he stumbled and fell back with a loud thud.

He winced, afraid that he might have woken someone up, but when he looked around, all of the others were still fast asleep. However, Nozos had been awake this whole time, and had been watching Gobulir's movements with interest. He had been curious as to what Gobulir was going to do with the jewels, and now he muttered to himself in quiet awe.

Gobulir's heart raced as he held the jewel in his hands, examining it closely in the moonlight. It was more beautiful than he had ever imagined, and he could not help but marvel at its radiance. He wondered how much it was worth, and what he could do with it. But as he looked back at the sleeping figures of his friends, he knew that he could not risk waking them up.

He carefully slipped the jewel into his pocket, making sure that it was secure. Then, he settled back into his watchful position, keeping an eye on the sleeping people around him. The night was still and quiet and Gobulir could feel the weight of the jewel in his pocket, a constant reminder of the secrets that he now held.

Gobulir stirred as the morning sun filtered through the clouds and shone in his eyes. He had fallen asleep while keeping watch and the guilt hit him like a punch to the gut. He had let everyone down, and now he would have to face their disappointment. He rubbed his eyes and sat up, feeling stiff and achy from sleeping on the hard ground.

As he blinked the sleep from his eyes, he saw Reibeala standing over him, a scowl on her face. "Gobulir, you were supposed to be keeping watch," she scolded him. "What happened?"

Gobulir groaned and rubbed the back of his neck. "I'm sorry, Reibeala. I don't know what happened. I was just so tired."

Reibeala rolled her eyes. "Well, it's a good thing nothing happened while you were asleep. We could have been attacked by that." She said whilst pointing over to where Kraken was.

Reibeala suddenly shouted for everyone to hear. "Gobulir, what happened to Kraken!? He's not here!" she exclaims. Gobulir, still groggy from sleep, struggled to open his eyes and comprehend what was going on.

"What do you mean he's gone?" Gobulir rubs his eyes, trying to clear his vision. "He was here last night, right?"

Alberad and Zerig quickly jumped up and started scanning the area for any signs of Kraken. They looked in every direction, but there was no sign of the massive creature.

"I don't get it," Toru said, scratching his head. "How could he just disappear like that, without waking us?"

"Maybe he wasn't as dead as we thought," Qyvrag suggested. "Maybe he got up and wandered off."

"No, that's not possible," Reibeala insisted. "We saw him die. There's no way he could've survived that."

As they continued to search for Kraken, gazing into the distance, the group started to become increasingly worried. They had defeated the monster and thought they were safe.

Triton spoke up calmly, "It's possible that Kraken dissolved like the mini Krakens did. He could have attacked us in our sleep but he didn't. So, I think we'll be fine. We have to trust that Kraken is gone for good."

Chapter 65

Beginning of Time

As they sat around the fire, feeling sorry for themselves and lamenting over the destruction caused by the war, Alberad suddenly stood up abruptly and walked off in sorrow. The rest of the group watched as he disappeared into the distance, wondering what he was up to.

Alberad couldn't take it anymore. He couldn't bear the sorrow and the hopelessness that hung in the air. He was hoping to find solace in his own thoughts.

He wandered aimlessly through the barren landscape, searching for some sign of hope. And then he saw it, a small green sprout pushing its way up through the rocky soil.

He approached the seedling with a mixture of curiosity and caution, marvelling at its resilience in the midst of such devastation. As he looked closer, he noticed the intricate details of its tiny leaves and delicate roots.

Alberad couldn't help but feel a glimmer of hope in his heart. Despite the destruction and chaos around them, life still found a way to push through. He knelt down and gently brushed the dirt away from the seedling, giving it room to grow.

He paused for a moment, admiring the tiny plant as it swayed gently in the breeze. For a moment, he forgot about the destruction and the hopelessness he felt. He thought about the seedling, and how it represented new life, and the possibility of growth and renewal.

After a few minutes, Alberad returned, a look of wonder and amazement on his face, feeling a glimmer of hope. "Hey everyone," he called out, "You won't believe what I just saw," he said, his voice shaking with excitement.

"What is it?" Cutter asked, intrigued.

"I just saw a little tree seedling back there. It's small, but it's a sign that life can still find a way, even in the midst of all this destruction."

The group looked at each other, surprised and slightly uplifted by Alberad's words. Perhaps there was still a glimmer of hope left in this world after all. They sat in silence, contemplating the significance of Alberad's discovery.

The group were still reeling from the destruction of their home and the loss of their friend Albwin. They were all feeling sorry for themselves, wallowing in the devastation of their once-beautiful land. Maldreg stood up, a determined look on his face.

"I know it seems like all hope is lost," he began, "but we mustn't forget that life goes on. We can't give up just because everything we had is gone. We must keep fighting and keep pushing forward, no matter what!"

The others looked up at him, surprised at his sudden optimism.

"And look around you," Maldreg continued, gesturing towards the broken mountains in the distance. "Sure, they're a mess now, but that's just the raw material we need to start rebuilding. You know what they say," he quipped, "if you can't fix it, that'll do!" The group laughed weakly, appreciating the attempt at humour.

A small smile started to spread across the faces of the group, and even Triton, who had been quiet for some time, looked up.

"You're right Maldreg," he said. "We can't just sit around here feeling sorry for ourselves. We need to start rebuilding and creating something new, something better."

Triton was inspired by Maldreg's words, he stood up with a determined look on his face. "Maldreg's right," he said, "there's hope for the future. We may have lost everything, but we still have each other, and that's something."

The others in the group looked at him with a mix of surprise and curiosity. Triton continued, "And where there's water, there's a home for the Aquanauts. We're not defeated yet. We'll find a way to rebuild, to start anew."

A glimmer of hope shining in their eyes now. "But we can't do it alone," Triton added. "We need to band together, to help each other out, and to make the best of what we have left."

Now looking around at each of his companions, who are all listening intently, Triton continued.

"We can do this," he said, his voice ringing with conviction. "We'll rebuild, we'll survive, and we'll thrive."

The group cheered, their spirits lifted by Triton's words. They may have lost everything, but they still have hope. And with that hope, they'll find a way to make a new life for themselves.

The positivity within the group was suddenly interrupted by the remaining Wyvinites. Without a word, they all stood up and began to fly away.

Confusion washed over the group, and Toru shouted out, "What's going on? Where are they going?"

Alvin replied, "I knew they would do that. They never wanted to be a part of this group anyway."

The Wyvinites continued to fly away, their silhouettes slowly disappearing into the distance. The group watched in silence, unsure of what to make of this sudden departure.

Reibeala spoke up, "We should have tried harder to include them. Maybe they could have helped us."

Triton replied with a sense of acceptance to the situation, "It's a shame. But we can't force anyone to stay. We'll have to make do with what we have."

Maldreg added, "We still have each other. And as long as we're together, there's always hope."

Chapter 66

Coming Together

As the group of Elvians, Mountaineers, and Aquanauts sat around the fire, they all began to share their thoughts about what the future held for them. It was clear that they had all been through a lot, but they were still hopeful that they could come together and build something better.

Reibeala spoke up first looking at the Elvians and Aquanauts, "We've all lost so much, but we still have each other. Maybe we can start over and build something new, something together."

They began to talk about how they could come together and rebuild their homes and communities. The Elvians offered their knowledge of their magic and their skills in nature and woodwork. The Mountaineers offered their expertise in building and crafting, and the Aquanauts offered their knowledge of water and marine life.

Together, they saw a path forward, a way to create a new and better future for themselves. They all agreed that they would need to work together, to share their knowledge and resources, and to never give up hope.

As the day wore on, the group continued to talk, planning and dreaming of what their new community could be like. They all felt a sense of purpose and determination, a new hope for the future.

As the group continued their discussion about their plans for the future, Triton spoke up and said, "We need to be vigilant. We don't know what else could be out there, and we can't let our guard down."

Maldreg pipped up and added, "Yes, we've already seen how dangerous it can be. We need to be prepared for anything."

Reibeala chimed in, "And we need to stick together. We're stronger as a group than we are as individuals."

Alberad agreed and said, "We can't let our differences divide us. We all want the same thing - a better future for ourselves and our families."

Keijo, who had been quiet for most of the discussion, spoke up and said, "I'll keep watch tonight. We can take turns keeping an eye out for any dangers."

The rest of the group all smiled and began to make plans for the future. They knew that they couldn't let their guard down, but they were hopeful for a better future together.

9 781916 981348